THRILLS ON ICE

BY AURELIA OSBORNE

Renaissance

THRILLS ON ICE ©2014 by Aurelia Osborne. All rights reserved. No part of this book may be used or reproduced in any manner whatsoever without written permission except in the case of brief quotations in critical articles and reviews. For more information, contact Renaissance Press. First edition.

Cover art by Caroline Frechette. Interior design by Natasha Brousseau. Editing by Kyle Bentley, Sanja Valentina Cimesa, and L. P. Vallee.

Legal deposit, Library and Archives Canada, October 2014.

ISBN 978-0-9936575-0-4

Renaissance Press

http://renaissancebookpress.com

info@renaissancebookpress.com

To Caroline. She knows why.

PROLOGUE

Oct 3rd (Associated Press)

Susanna Miles, the star of Canadian figure skating, prepares for her next season. Miles' performance has made her an invaluable asset to the Canadian figure skating legacy, and her dedication has won her three world championships and one silver medal at the Vancouver Olympics. Already, there is talk of another medal in Russia. Perhaps gold this time? Miles' first competition this year is Skate America [Oct 19-21] which is part of the prestigious Grand Prix.

Oct 3rd (skatersCAN.tumblr.com)

So Canada's sweetheart, Susanna Miles, is finally ready to begin her 2012-2013 season. About time, since other skaters have been competing for almost a month. Why the delay? Is it the glamour of being an Olympian, and all the privileges that come with it? Is it that the rumors of conflict between her choreographer and her notoriously protective manager

1

and mother are true? But in the end, who cares, really? The important part is that SHE'S BACK! It's so good to see you, Suzie. Or to be seeing you on Oct 19th, anyway. (I tease because I care, bb.)

Email

From: Olivia Miles
To: Susanna Miles
October 3rd, at 19:00

Did you see that? [link to the blog entry] I hope that this rumor about the choreographer didn't come from you, I've taught you better than to talk to those amateur gossip rags.

Email

From: Susanna Miles
To: Olivia Miles
October 3rd, at 19:06

I didn't talk to them, mother. I didn't need to, the fight you had with Aaron was pretty public, and pretty loud.

How goes the search for a new choreographer, btw?

Email

From: Olivia Miles
To: Susanna Miles
October 3rd, at 19:11

You don't have to concern yourself with that. Just focus on your skating.

Email

From: Susanna Miles
To: Olivia Miles
October 3rd, at 19:14

You know, I've had some ideas about choreography. I've talked it over with Liam, and he says I could be on to something.

Email

From: Olivia Miles
To: Susanna Miles
October 3rd, at 19:19

I've already told you Susanna, your job is to skate. Let someone else worry about the other details. If you let yourself get distracted, the quality of your work will suffer. I will find you a choreographer, you just focus on your training.

Email

From: Susanna Miles
To: Olivia Miles
October 3rd, at 19:21

Yes, mother.

Oct 15, 2012 (Associated Press)

Susanna Miles' management team announced today that she has dropped out of Skate America. There has been no word as to when Miles can be expected back on the ice. No further comments were issued.

Oct 16, 2012 (skatersCAN.tumblr.com)

OMG, you guys. Susanna Miles dropped her whole calendar. You know what this means, don't you? She got injured, and it's serious. She could have a broken bone (makes 'break a leg' look like a stupid expression for 'good luck' doesn't it?) or a torn ACL. Either way, her season is pretty much over. And it could be worse than that. Her whole career could be over. Can you imagine a world where we can't watch Susanna Miles skate ever again? That's too terrible for words. You stay strong, honey! We love you!

Email

From: Thaddeus Bancroft, MD
To: Olivia Miles
November 16th at 10:45

I regret to inform you, Madame, that your daughter's recovery was greatly set back by yesterday's incident. After examining her, it is now my professional assessment that she will no longer be able to compete. With considerable care, in time, she may be able to walk without a brace, but little more can be expected.

Email

From: Adrian Kirby, MD
To: Olivia Miles
December 22nd at 13:30

Mrs. Miles, I must admit that I find your request somewhat troubling. It is not the usual practice to challenge the diagnosis of a colleague. However, if you are determined, and if you and your daughter are able to make the journey to Winnipeg, I would be happy to examine her. I'm afraid my private practice does not allow me the luxury to make house calls in Toronto. I have some time after the holidays. You may contact me via this email address to make further arrangements.

Email

From: Olivia Miles
To: Susanna Miles
December 22nd at 13:36

Can you believe the NERVE of the man? Us, go to Winnipeg? I'd rather die than go back there.

Email

From: Susanna Miles
To: Olivia Miles
December 22nd at 13:45

Then let me go alone. Let's face it, mother, we don't have a lot of options. It took you a whole month to even find a doctor willing to look at my knee. They won't let me compete until a medical professional signs the okay. So it's either I go to Winnipeg, or I don't have a career anymore.

Email

From: Olivia Miles
To: Susanna Miles
December 22nd at 15:02

Fine. I'll make the arrangements.

CHAPTER 1

The flight left Toronto just after eight o'clock, with a delay of approximately thirty minutes. Considering that I had to go through security in crutches and that I had to be there an hour and a half early, my day has already lasted forever. Or at least, that's what it feels like.

The good news is that Mom's not on the plane with me right now. I never thought I would hear myself say this, but the break is probably going to do us both some good. She's always been there for me, and I've always been grateful for that. Someone has to manage my career, schedule competitions, deal with sponsors, handle money, find the best people, from the coach to the choreographer to the costume designer, and so on and so forth. I'm glad it's not me, because I don't think I could handle the workload. I'm glad to let my mom handle all that. I just want to skate.

Things have been different for the last couple of years, though. She's been more intense, I guess. She's always been determined, but now it's worse. She has to get her way, on everything, all the time. It took her over a month to accept that I wasn't faking my injury, or milking it, making it sound worse than it was, or something. When my doctor told her I might never skate again, she threw a fit like I've never seen from her before. It was kind of scary. Then she went looking for a second opinion. At this point, thankfully, she's pretty much admitted to herself that this season is shot to hell. It's the first time in a long time she didn't get her way.

Now she's thinking about next season. Olympic season. My last chance at an Olympic gold medal.

Me, I'm thinking about my future, trying to figure out what I'm going to do with the rest of my life.

My mom believes that this Dr. Kirby I'm going to meet will give her the news she wants to hear, that he can magically get me back in competitive shape for this fall. I don't think it's going to happen. Dr. Bancroft is the sports injury specialist in Toronto, as if my mother would send me to anyone else. If he says I'm done, who am I to argue?

So here's what I think is going to happen: Dr. Kirby will confirm that my career is over. I'll call my mom to tell her, she'll complain and call me lazy, unmotivated, ungrateful, careless, incompetent, and all those lovely little nicknames I've picked up since October, and then... I have no idea. That's what I need to figure out.

I've been skating for as long as I can remember. I don't really know anything else. I got a GED, working with tutors, because when you're traveling all over the world between September and April to compete, school is kind of problematic. Most skaters, especially the really good ones, become coaches after their pro career is over. But I don't think I would be comfortable having that kind of authority over someone. I could be a teacher, I guess, but I've never been around children much. I don't know if I have the patience. That leaves me with some shitty minimum wage job, and I don't even know if you can live on a minimum wage job. I've heard that you can't.

I still have the sponsorship deals. Even if I don't compete anymore the fact that I've been to the Olympics means my name still has some buying power, so I should be able to keep a few of those, for a while. That should be enough to make a living, especially considering I won't have to pay for a coach, and rent a rink for training, and all that. But then again I've never really handled money: that was my mother's job. I don't know if I really can keep the deals, or how much they are worth. I know that money from the sponsors goes into the account, and then back out to pay for everything else, but I don't know the numbers.

I suppose I'll have to ask her. If I don't have a career anymore, I don't need my career managed, so she could turn the accounts back to me. That is one discussion I am not looking forward to. It's almost enough to make me just give up on the accounts, and get that minimum wage job and go on with the rest of my life. But, on the other hand, there would be no money from sponsors if I hadn't been out skating for it. I really don't know what to do.

I'm hoping Winnipeg will be some source of inspiration. I'm not really sure how; I mean my mom and I left for Toronto when I was nine years old, and even before then I wasn't doing much other than skating. I'd already won a few regional competitions. My dad doesn't even live there anymore; he got a job in Nanaimo after the divorce, and I've barely heard from him since then. But the fact that Dr. Kirby is in Winnipeg, and that he said I must go to him to get his opinion... it seems like a sign.

I guess I'll figure it out. I don't have much of a choice anyway. At least I know for sure that, as long as I stay in Winnipeg, I won't have to deal with my mother face-to-face. For some reason I don't understand, and don't care about that much to be honest, she hates Winnipeg.

The plane touches down. Time to get on my way then.

***

The flight from Denver took forever but, finally, the team is back home. At least for a little while. The schedule is really rough, because the season started two weeks late, but we're still playing the same amount of games and we're still finishing on the same date. It's like when we play the year of the winter Olympics. Like next year. I get tired just thinking about it.

At least we won. That was good.

But then there was a celebration, then the plane ride at shit-o-clock this morning, crossing a time zone, and then training all day for the game tomorrow...

Still, I'm not bitching. I'm a professional. I give my team and my game everything, and I plan on doing that all the way to June, when we win the playoffs. Then I'll crash for two months until pre-season camp for the next season.

Better than sitting behind some desk all year long, with only two weeks of vacation.

Reporters are waiting for us at the gate, as usual. And they want to talk to me, which is... well, not usual, but, you know, frequent.

"Luke! You got another Star of the Game last night. Collecting them or something?"

"I don't know about that," I answer. "If they want to keep giving me these Stars, I guess I'll just have to do my best to keep earning them."

"We're halfway through the season, and you boys are in eighth place. Think you can make it to the playoffs?"

"We'll see."

"All right, that's enough," the coach interrupts. "The boys have had a long night, and a long flight. Let's give them some space, all right folks?" He drags me away and, once we're out of the reporter's hearing range, he turns to me. "What'd I say about talking to them?"

"Come on, Coach. They were right there, talking. I couldn't ignore them, it would be rude. What'd I say that was so bad, anyway?"

"Nothing today, maybe, but one day you'll open your mouth without thinking and get us all in a lot of trouble. Just get yourself back home, change and shower. Back on the ice at one."

"Yes, Coach."

I make my way to the baggage claim. Once there, I find a very pleasant surprise: a cute, short girl with brown hair in a braid and her left knee in a brace. She's struggling to grab her suitcase and her backpack while holding on to her crutches.

Time to be chivalrous.

"Excuse me, miss. Would you like me to help you?"

She turns around to face me. Her green eyes widen and she catches her breath. I can read the signs: she wants me. I don't think she recognizes me, though. Not a hockey fan, I guess. That's all right, I can always convert her.

She takes a sharp breath, squares her shoulders. She's going to try and tell me that she doesn't need help. The independent type, then. Nothing wrong with that. Besides, if she's got any smarts, she'll realize that she can't actually grab all of her stuff without help. Shouldn't there be someone with her already? It's not like she can drive herself, not with that knee.

She looks at her baggage and sighs. She is smart, then. "Yes," she says. "I would like some help. In fact, if you could just..."

She hands her crutches to me before bending down to grab her backpack, then fixes it solidly on her shoulders. She also grabs the purse on her suitcase and straps it on. She has a good sense of equilibrium, doing all of this with her weight on just one leg. I wonder how flexible she is.

14

She looks at her suitcase, like she's trying to figure out a way to drag it while using her crutches. Sounds like a plan to hurt herself to me. I better step up. Fortunately, my equipment bag is just coming up on the luggage belt. I hand her back her crutches.

"Here. Let me take this." I grab her suitcase with one hand, and my bag with the other.

"Oh!" she says. "You're a hockey player."

"I am." I knew she hadn't recognized me.

"Should I know you? I'm sorry, I don't follow hockey, really."

"It's okay. Maybe someday I can convince you to give it a try?" I avoid her question, on purpose. It could be nice, starting a relationship with a girl who doesn't know that I'm Lucas Crawford, superstar of the Winnipeg Jets. I drop her suitcase and extend my hand for a shake. "I'm Luke."

"I'm Anna." We shake hands. She has freckles. Not a lot of them, but enough that you notice. I never realized before how god-damned adorable freckles are. I can't stop staring at hers. I must have been staring for too long, though, because she gets uncomfortable and yanks her hand back. Whoops.

"Well... I should-"

"Right," I add, grabbing her suitcase once more. "So, is there someone meeting you?"

"Um, no," she answers. "I'm here alone. I was just going to grab a cab."

"Okay." We begin to walk toward the cab station, me one step behind her. "So, you're taking a vacation alone with a broken leg?"

"It's not a break, it's a tear. And I'm not taking a vacation, I'm moving in. Moving back, I should say."

"Well, that's cool." More opportunities to meet each other, to play the dating game more slowly. I have a feeling this girl would prefer slowly. "I just moved in two years ago myself. It's a great town."

"Yeah, I think so too." We're reaching the doors. Anna pulls out some green mittens, matching her green hat, from her coat pockets and puts them on. The coat isn't designer or fur or anything that I can see, it's just a black winter coat. Black coat, black boots, plain jeans, knitted hat and mittens; it all says 'practical girl', not 'fashionista.' My sister would be so disappointed.

There's a free cab just ahead. She flags it, and the driver comes out to put her suitcase in the trunk. I think about staying around, close enough to hear where she's going, but that would be way too stalkerish. Still, I better find a way to get in touch with her. Winnipeg isn't that small, who knows if we'll ever bump into each other again.

"Hey, do you know a place called Goodman's, on Salter?"

She hesitates. "I could find it. Why?"

"I'm meeting a group of friends there Monday night, about seven. You could come."

"Yeah," she nods shyly. "I could come." Then she hops in the cab and disappears.

Oh, yeah, she'll be there.

CHAPTER 2

I'm primed and ready when I get home. The high that comes with successfully flirting with a pretty girl lasts exactly as long as it takes me to walk through the door and pick up my mail. There's a bright red envelope, postmarked Montreal, among all the bills. It contains a generic Christmas card with a schmaltzy message and the signature "Dad". That's it.

Of course, it's exactly what I've come to expect from dear old dad; a Christmas card almost two weeks late. Doesn't make it any less of a downer, though.

I pick up my cell and call my sister, the same thing I do every time I hear from dad. I'm not sure why; she gets pretty much the same messages at pretty much the same time. And if she didn't, if she got something I didn't get, do I really need the proof that she's the favorite? And what happens if I got something and she didn't? It would feel like I'm rubbing it in her face, and it's the last thing I want to do.

I know all that, but I'm calling her anyway.

She doesn't pick up, so I leave a message. "Hey, Ava, it's Luke. So I just came home, I'll be here for about a week. I was thinking we could do something, meet the gang at Goodman's on Monday, I don't have a game then. Also, I just found dad's Christmas card in my mail, wondering if you got yours. Call me back."

She does call me back, in the middle of my practice, of course. We're taking a quick break, so I take a chance and answer the phone.

"About time, sis."

"Don't start with me, bro. I'm totally swamped at work today. I am currently talking to you while driving back home to pick up some specs I forgot there this morning. Do you realize I'm breaking the law for you? I hope you're happy. You know, owning and operating your own business is hard.

It's not like you, boys chasing boys on ice nine months out of the year."

"I'm not even going to pretend that you don't know hockey is a lot more than that."

"Just because you like to hit each other doesn't make it hard. It just means that there's a surplus of testosterone."

It's an argument we've had many times before, and I just don't have that kind of time, or the amount of beer necessary for it. "So, about dad?"

"Yes, I got his Christmas card. No, it didn't say anything that yours didn't also say, I'm sure. Honestly, Luke, you need to develop a better attitude about this. That's just the way he is. If you want to talk to him, and I know you do, you have to make the first step."

That's another conversation I don't have enough beer for. Actually, better switch the beer to hard liquor for that one. "And about Monday?"

"Yeah, sure, we can go to Goodman's on Monday. I'll talk to Chuck, work on getting everyone together. Anything special I should know?"

"I've kind of already invited someone. A girl." That might have been a mistake to say out loud, but since Anna's coming Ava is sure to find out about it. "It was casual, you know," I add after a minute of Ava saying nothing. "She might not even come." But I'm sure she will.

"Luke, you've invited a girl out for drinks and you want me to be there to meet her? This is, like, girlfriend territory. You're finally moving on after that bitch Talia. I'm so proud."

There's not enough alcohol in the world for that conversation. Plus the break is almost over. "Hey, sis, I gotta..."

"What the hell?"

"What?!"

"Not you. There's a moving van blocking up my parking space. I gotta go. See ya Monday."

And she hangs up just as I was about to. She always does that. I don't know how, but she does. Maybe she's psychic or something.

But I don't have time to think about that right now; it's time to go back to the ice. So back to the ice I go, and I try to focus on the practice, like the professional I am. But, well, I'm thinking about Anna, and I'm thinking about Talia, and I'm thinking about my dad, and I'm not paying enough attention to the goon who's charging me, and I get rammed into the barriers.

Shit, that hurts.

***

My day has officially taken a turn for the worse. The trip itself had brought up some cautious sense of optimism in me, and then there was meeting Luke. I mean, having a really good looking guy flirt with you is bound to pick you up. Nothing's going to come out of it, of course. I'm just not in the right mindset for dating; I've got too much going on in my life right now. I don't have a lot of dating experience - or, actually, no dating experience at all - and I suspect that now would be a bad time to learn.

Besides, Monday is the day of my meeting with Doctor Kirby, and who knows how I'll be feeling afterward. Although I might go to that place, Goodman's. I wonder, is it a pub or a club or a bar or what? Anyway, it's a group of people meeting up, so it's not like a date, so I might go. Or not. I'll figure out how I feel the day of.

The point is, leaving the airport, I was feeling pretty good. The cab took me to the apartment my mother chose for me, and I was pleasantly surprised. It's lovely, located on the first floor, which is best considering my current predicament and the lack of elevators. It's a bit on the small side; one bedroom, one bathroom, a kitchen and a den. But let's face it, I've lived in the Olympic Village. This is all the space I need.

So I was feeling pretty good by the time the delivery men arrived with my furniture. They took care of that in a hurry. Turns out that the extra installation fees includes putting the furniture in the room where it belongs, pulling the plastic sheet off the couch, and that is pretty much it.

"Look, let's just use some logic here. I have a knee brace, which means I can't bend my knee. I'm in crutches, you see that right? How am I supposed to assemble furniture like that?"

"You could call someone to help you."

"I don't know anyone here." I used to, once upon a time, but who knows where those people are nowadays. And there's no point bringing this up and confusing the man even more. "I'm just moving into town right now, can't you tell? Isn't the fact that the apartment is absolutely empty a big enough clue?"

"Who just moves to a town where they don't know anybody? Don't you realize it ain't safe?"

I don't even know how to respond to that. What does that have to do with his breach of contract? And who does he think he is anyway?

"You're not here to judge my lifestyle. You are here to install my furniture, like you said you would in that contract I signed."

"We fulfilled our contractual obligations to the letter, miss."

"But there's a spirit to those obligations. Would it kill you to do more than the bare minimum?"

"Excuse me." I turn toward the door and see a girl standing there. She looks much taller than I am. I'm used to people being taller than me, it would be hard not to be since I'm only five foot one. She's seriously taller than I am, though, by at least six inches, I'd say. She's pretty, too, with dark skin, short black hair and very sharp features. "It appears that your van is blocking my parking space."

"Sorry, ma'am. We'll get right out of your way."

"No you won't," I reply quickly. "We're not done here."

"We're already late, miss. Have a good day."

"Wait a minute!" I run after the delivery men, forgetting that one of my legs is currently in less than optimal condition, and I end up flat on my face. I look up to see the delivery men walk right out of the door. Jerks! And now my leg is aching really badly. The exhaustion and the pain and the frustration are just a bit too much. I let my head fall back on the floor, with my eyes tearing up.

"I guess I have really bad timing, huh?" I look up once more. The girl is kneeling next to me. She looks so sad, like it's her fault those guys were lazy assholes. "Do you need some help?"

"Yeah. Yeah, I do."

She pulls me up on my feet and half-carries me to the couch. Wow, she's strong.

"I'm Ava, by the way. Ava Crawford. I live two floors above."

"Nice to meet you. I'm Anna Miles. I just got into town this morning."

"Some welcome, right?"

"Well, I talked to other people before. People in the airport, and the cab driver. And you look pretty nice so far."

"I try. So, you mind if I take a look around, see what needs to be done?"

"Be my guest."

She quickly walks around the apartment. "Is that all you have?" She asks when she comes back to the den.

"My boxes are coming later this afternoon."

Ava lets out a sigh. "Okay. I'm going to need some muscle." She picks up her cell, and dials.

"Hey, Jeannine, I need you to take over for the afternoon. Something came up. I'll fax those specs in a minute, and you can handle the meeting. Push everything that can wait back to tomorrow, and just handle the rest, all right? I'm counting on you."

She hangs up and dials again.

"Hey Chuck. You wanna come to apartment 1 in our building, and bring the tools? We've got a new neighbor, and she needs help getting settled in. She's in crutches. Yeah. The guys are in practice right now. We can call them in a couple of hours, I guess. Or we can manage by ourselves. Okay then, see you in a minute."

Ava hangs up. "She didn't complain half as much as I thought she would about closing the shop in the middle of the day. Guess things are slow."

"She?"

"Yeah, Chuck, the girl I just called. She's my roommate. She owns a garage that specializes in older cars. I would also call our boyfriends and my brother, but I know that they're busy right now. I need to go fax those specs. I'll be back in a few minutes, okay?"

I nod and watch her leave. Apparently my move has been taken over by my neighbor Ava and a girl called Chuck. Might as well just go with it.

Chuck arrives just after Ava comes back, and I learn a few things. She is less intimidating than Ava physically; closer to my own height, with long curly brown hair, gray eyes and a heart-shaped face. She is, however, much more intimidating than Ava, personality-wise. She introduces herself as Charlotte Kirby, and when I react to the name, for obvious reasons, she stares daggers at me.

"If you're even thinking about comparing me to that pink marshmallow nightmare, I swear to God..."

"What? No, it's just... I've got an appointment on Monday with a Dr. Kirby."

That softens her up. "Oh, my dad. So your knee, it's a sport injury?"

I wonder how she guessed, and then I figure it out and feel stupid. Dr. Kirby is a sports injury specialist, and of course she would know that. "Yeah. Torn ACL. Last October."

Both Ava and Charlotte (I'm not calling her Chuck until she tells me to, not even in my head) grimace at the news.

"You guys look like you know something about that?"

"We're both dating hockey players," Ava says. "Between them, my brother and Chuck's dad, we've heard so many horror stories."

Charlotte slaps her hands together. "So, let's get you settled, then."

After a few hours and the assembly of the smaller, lighter furniture, they call their boyfriends and Ava's brother to help with the heavier stuff. Two guys eventually come knocking on my door. They are both over six feet tall, and muscular, and a very pleasant sight to see. The blond haired, blue eyed one introduces himself as Dominik, Ava's boyfriend. The dark haired, brown eyed one introduces himself as Pierce, Charlotte's boyfriend. Ava's brother is apparently nowhere to be seen, which upsets her.

"Where is he?"

"He got injured at practice, today," answers Dominik. "Nothing serious, but he's taking it easy before the game tomorrow."

"Well, that doesn't mean he can't come and help. Didn't that rocket guy do that once? Move after getting injured in a game?"

"It was the other way around, Aves," answers Pierce. "The Rocket played after getting injured moving into a new place."

"Besides, it was the forties, before there was insurance, and a players' union," adds Dominik.

"And, in case you never noticed," continues Pierce, "The Rocket was nuts. Like, genuinely crazy."

"Look at the old pictures; it's in the eyes," explains Dominik.

"Whatever. I still think he's a wimp, and I'm going to tell him exactly that on Monday."

"What's Monday?" asks Charlotte.

"My wimp of a brother and I are planning a little get-together. He asked a girl, and I think he doesn't want to freak her out, so he's making it a group outing instead of a romantic date."

"He's dating again? About damn time!"

"I know, right?"

The conversation is now just way too far over my head, so I speak up. "Um, what are you talking about?"

"Long story short?" Says Ava, "my brother's ex is a bitch, and we're glad he's moving on. Hey, you want to come on Monday?"

"I don't know. I would feel weird barging in on the date of a guy I've never met before. Besides, my plans on Monday kind of depend on what Dr. Kirby says." And on whether or not I gather up the nerve to go meet Luke at Goodman's.

My boxes arrive at this moment. Ava signs for the delivery so I don't have to leave the couch. The guys carry the boxes inside. I'm suddenly really glad to have two big strong guys here. Makes the whole thing a hell of a lot quicker.

"Your whole life fits in nine boxes?" Asks Ava.

"What? There's only supposed to be eight boxes." I grab my backpack, where I keep the list of which things are in what boxes, and indeed, there's only supposed to be eight boxes.

"Your whole life fits in eight boxes!?"

"Well, the plan was to buy the things I would need but couldn't pack, like cookware, electronics and decorative stuff. This is mostly clothes, books, things like that."

Ava still looks shocked. After a few minutes, she says, "on one hand, I applaud your sense of organization. On the other hand, I am so taking you shopping tomorrow."

"All right, as long as we make a detour by a hair salon." I take off my hat and show her the roots. I stopped dying my hair in November, after we talked to Dr. Bancroft. I never liked my hair brown, but my mother said it looked better on camera. Then again, I won't be on camera anymore, will I? "I want to go back to my original color."

"Cool. We're almost done here, we can make plans afterwards."

About an hour later, we're left with nothing but the mystery box.

"What should I do?"

"You should open it." Pierce's tone when he answers my question makes it clear he thinks the answer is obvious.

"But I'm sure that it's actually someone else's stuff. I can't just open it, it might be private, and then how would I get it back to them?"

"Maybe your parents or your friends packed a surprise box for you," Charlotte replies. "And if that's not it, if it really belongs to someone else, Ava or I can always get tape from our place and close it back up. Then you can call the moving company to try and figure out who it belongs to."

What Charlotte says makes sense, but it mostly goes in one ear and out the other. To be specific, everything after "a surprise box".

Oh, God. Tell me she didn't. Please.

I carefully open the box. I find myself staring at my face, in glossy magazine cover form. I can see sequins nestled behind, and I think I see my skates, too.

She did.

I try to shut the box, but Ava moves quicker than I can, and she grabs the magazine.

"Oh, my God. You're Susanna Miles. I can't believe I didn't recognize you, I'm such a huge fan. Why didn't you say something?"

"There's no point." A piece of paper catches my eye, I grab it. It's a message from my mom. "Just in case," it says. Thanks a lot, mother.

"Of course there's a point. You've accomplished all those wonderful things. You've been to the Olympics!"

"Yeah, and then I busted my knee, and my doctor in Toronto says I can't compete anymore. So the point is what, exactly?" I crumple the note and toss it away, before crossing my arms over my chest. Childish behavior, I know, but I can't help it.

"Anna," Ava says softly, "just because you can't do it anymore doesn't take away from what you've done. Aren't you proud of yourself?"

That's a good question. Am I proud of myself? Should I be? I was just doing the job. But I don't think I could explain it to Ava and the others. Instead I say: "I just don't want to dwell on it. It's over, I should move on."

"Maybe it's not, though," Charlotte says. "You are meeting my dad, after all."

"I don't expect him to tell me anything different."

"Well," Ava says, "even if you never skate again, it doesn't matter. I'm still so grateful to know you, because I think you are amazing."

Plenty of people have said that to me before, but the context always made it clear that they meant "your skating is amazing". Ava is the first one in a long time, maybe the first one ever, to make me feel that I am the one who's amazing. I smile at her.

"So," Dominik asks. "What do you want to do with that box?"

"Just stick it in a closet somewhere, okay?" If I try to send it back, my mom is only going to mail it to me again.

I want it out of my sight, and hopefully out of my mind. Dominik does as I ask and after making sure I would be okay for the night, they make their way out. Charlotte offers to drive me to meet her dad on Monday, the boys give me their phone numbers, in case I need anything, and Ava gives me a hug. "I think we'll get along really well."

She might be right.

The day didn't turn out so bad after all.

CHAPTER 3

Charlotte is there, knocking on my door bright and early on Monday morning. Good thing I'm ready for her. We leave for the hospital together.

"Thanks, Charlotte. It's nice of you to take the time off to drive me," I say when I can't bear the silence anymore.

"That's all right, I have people who can take care of the shop while I take the occasional morning and/or afternoon off. Besides, most of my clients are car collectors, who want to keep their old sports cars in shape for competing season. Those cars are stored away in the winter, typically. So these days, I only keep a couple of guys around for emergencies. And I get to play the good daughter by stopping by and seeing daddy at work. For the future, though, you better get a car."

"Apparently, I have one waiting for me." Another thing arranged by my mother. "Would you mind dropping me at the dealership after the appointment?"

"No, it's alright. Where is it?"

I fish around in my purse until I find the printed e-mail from my mother, with the name and address of the dealership. I read it out to Charlotte. She whistles.

"What?"

"That's a luxury dealership. They sell Mercedes, Cadillacs, Jaguars, things like that."

"Oh, God, mom." I sigh. "Well, she'll have to curtail her spending habits eventually, because the well is about to dry up."

"That's kinda harsh, Suzie Q."

"Please don't call me that."

"Why? You don't like that song?"

"I like the song fine, I just don't like the sound of Sue, or Suzie. I like Anna."

"Why not Susanna, other than for keeping your super Olympic star status a secret?"

"Mostly, it's what my mother calls me."

"... when you're in trouble?"

"No, pretty much all the time. I just wanted a change."

"Well, Charlotte is what my mother calls me when I'm in trouble. Why don't you call me Chuck, like everyone?"

"I was waiting for permission."

Charlotte explodes with laughter at this, even though it's true. "You have it," she finally says after catching her breath.

"Okay. So, why Chuck?"

"Well, when I was about seven, a boy called Charles moved into our old neighborhood. Some people started calling him Chuck and since Charles and Charlotte are kind of the same, I wanted to be called Chuck, too. He told me I couldn't, because it was a boy name and I was a girl. I punched him and broke his nose. My dad made me a deal then, I could be Chuck as long as I never started another fight."

"And so you've never been in a fight since?"

"None that I started, which was all I promised and all that could be expected of me. And we're here."

***

I end up spending almost seven hours at the hospital taking test after test. At least Dr. Kirby's very nice. He stops by in between tests to chat with me, to explain exactly what they're going to do, and to pass the time while he's waiting for test results.

He looks pleasantly surprised to learn that Chuck and I live in the same building and he shares some childhood stories about her, asks me about Toronto, and we compare our favorite Winnipeg haunts. I learn that the movie theater I used to go to as a kid is closed, but that my favorite restaurant is still open, and that the Kirbys like it too. Chuck proposes that we all go there sometime, and that I should meet her mother.

Finally, late in the afternoon, Dr. Kirby and I go back to his office. Chuck went back to the shop a while ago, after we agreed that I would call her when this was over so we could go to the dealership.

"Well, Anna," Dr Kirby says. "I bet you can't wait to hear the diagnosis."

"Actually, I'm pretty sure I already know the diagnosis. Dr. Bancroft was pretty definitive."

"I know, that's why I found the results so surprising, and why I've kept you here almost all day. I was trying to find the cause of that diagnosis. I didn't."

"I'm sorry, what?"

"Your leg is exactly at the level I would expect it to be, considering the nature and date of your injury and your course of treatment. Not back to one hundred percent, of course, but on the way there for sure. My recommendation would be to keep your current regimen, to start meeting with a local physiotherapist, and to resume training in increments. I'll set up another appointment with you in April, when I believe you'll be ready for full competitive training again."

Back to full competitive training. By April. The current season's still shot, but it means three months until the beginning of the next season. Six months before the first competitions. Ten months before the Olympics. It could all still happen.

Well, shit. My mother had been right. What now?

"Anna?" Dr Kirby asks. "Are you still there?"

"Yes, sorry. It's just... so much, you know. So unexpected. I'm not sure what to think."

"Well, let's take it one step at a time. For now, let's take that brace off and retire the crutches, all right? I'll give you the name of a physiotherapist I work with a lot. I want you to make an appointment as soon as possible. He might be closed by now, it is a bit late after all. But I want you there tomorrow morning, all right?"

***

A bit later, Chuck and I go by the dealership and pick up the horrible, enormous, gold Mercedes SUV my mother chose for me. It must be the most expensive car in the lot, and I hate it. I can't imagine how my mom would find such a nice, perfect little apartment, and such a terrible monstrosity of a car. I guess it's something to do with the fact that no one will come in my apartment, but people will see me driving around. I tried asking if a trade was possible, and the dealer looked at me like I had sprouted another head, so I guess I'm stuck with it.

We go by the physiotherapist's office, which is indeed closed, and then go home. Chuck goes to get ready for the night out with Ava and her brother, while I go to call my mother.

"April?! What do you mean, April?"

"I mean the month after March, mom."

"Don't take that tone with me, Susanna. It's only three months until the season starts. How are you supposed to get back to full shape with only three months of training and six months of sitting on your butt before that?"

"Mom! I haven't been sitting on my butt. I've been injured..."

"You've been coddled."

"And I'm sure that I'll be back on the ice before April. It just won't be competitive levels of training. I'll be taking it slow, for a bit, that's all."

"What else is new? I expect you to call me every day with a report of your progress. And I expect there to be progress, Susanna. No lolly-gagging."

"Yes, mother," I answer to the dial tone. I think she might have been over-compensating for her lack of physical presence in my life with extra aggression. Either way, the phone call has left me drained.

I remember that Luke is waiting for me at Goodman's on Salter street. That he had helped me with my luggage and flirted. That he is big and strong, but not intimidating. I remember the way his smile shone against his copper skin, the teasing warmth in his dark eyes.

And still, I only have the energy to walk to my bedroom, strip off my jeans and pull the covers over my head.

***

She didn't come. It's getting close to midnight, and we're about to call the party off and go home. She's not coming. She's not late, stuck in traffic somewhere. She just didn't come.

Did I misread the signals? Should I have been more insistent? Should I have given her my number, or asked for hers? Would she have agreed?

The worst part is that my blabbermouth sister had told everyone about "the girl." The boys worked out the timing and figured I met her in the airport, so she became "airport girl." The whole gang spent the first half-hour teasing me about "airport girl," but as time went on, the teasing slowed, and then stopped, and now I can see the pity in their eyes. It's a nightmare.

Why didn't she come, though? I don't get it. Did something happen? Did I do something wrong?

I should just forget her, right? There are other girls. It didn't work with that one, move on to the next.

But why didn't she come?

CHAPTER 4

The week passes. On Tuesday I have breakfast with Ava and Chuck. Ava mostly wanted someone to vent to about the fact that the girl her brother was supposed to meet didn't show up. Chuck is apparently sick of the subject. I'm sympathetic, as much as I can be considering that I really don't know Ava's brother at all, but it makes me feel a little guilty too. I can't help but imagine Luke, sitting in some bar, waiting for me, and me not showing up.

Well, Monday night was just a bad night for me. I would have called to let him know, but I didn't have his phone number. And if he was really interested in me, he would have given me his phone number, right? He probably didn't wait up for me at all. When he saw I wasn't coming, he probably found another girl. A prettier, more interesting girl. I'm not that big a deal, anyway. Not when I'm not skating.

So, anyway, after breakfast Chuck goes back to the shop, while Ava announces that she has taken the day off to show me around the neighborhood. We go to the physiotherapist, Caleb Johnson, who sets me up with regular appointments. He also seems really nice. Then she helps me find all the little things that make a neighborhood special; the 24-hour coffee shops, the little specialty stores, the nearest delivery places and unknown restaurants, etc. Most importantly, she shows me the nearest arena where I can start training when the time comes. As it happens it's my childhood arena, the one where I won my first competitions.

We also go on the promised shopping trip. At the time, I didn't realize that she also meant to buy me new clothes. The clothes I already had were fine, or so I thought anyway. It turns out that Ava had a weakness for clothes. We also bought apartment-related stuff, so I let her go on her fashion kick. It wasn't too bad; she has good taste.

She also tries to cheer me up about my new, horrible car, by telling me that at least it has a lot of space in the back. That's nice of her, even if it doesn't really work. I don't exactly need a lot of space.

So, between the settling in, the physiotherapy three times a week, the daily phone calls to my mother, and spending time with my two new friends, time flies relatively quickly. Before I know it, it's Friday. There's a game in town tonight, against the Devils. The girls both have season tickets, since their boyfriends play for the Jets, but they also purchase extra tickets occasionally. They did tonight. Both of Chuck's parents will be there, and the girls want me to come too.

I don't have any problem with going to a hockey game. I have some difficulties with the outfit Ava's trying to convince me to wear.

"In the name of God, Ava, why?"

"Because I want my brother to notice you. He's finally ready to move on from his bitch of an ex we all hate and since things didn't work out with the girl from Monday, I figure it's a sign. I like you, you're my new best friend, and I love my brother, so you're going to wear this cute little outfit I'm setting out for you and after the game, we're all going to meet the boys up at the lockers and go out for drinks, and you two are going to start dating and eventually live happily ever after."

"Ava, that is not how reality works."

"That's how my reality works. Now come on, get dressed."

"For the last time, I am not putting this outfit on. I can't wear a t-shirt and a leather jacket to the arena, I'll freeze. And I can't wear those boots. I'm not supposed to put stress on my legs, and look at those heels!"

"All right, I'll give you the boots, although I can't imagine why you bought them if you aren't going to wear them."

"I am going to wear them, later, when my knee is stronger. Like this spring. Those aren't winter boots anyway, look: there's no lining, no fur or insulation, nothing to keep my feet warm. I would freeze my toes wearing those outside tonight."

"What is it with that obsession with freezing? You wore a lot less than that when you were competing. In an arena. On the ice. Which is, by definition, cold."

"I was skating when I was competing. Physical exercise keeps you warm, it's a well-known fact."

Chuck, who had walked out of the room soon after the argument first broke out, walks back in and throws something at me. It's a long-sleeved shirt of thin white cotton.

"There. You can wear that under your t-shirt. With that, the jacket, your mittens and hat, and a huge cup of coffee, you should be fine. Plus my dad will be there, so if you start to feel the symptoms of hypothermia, he can rush you to the hospital. Now, please, can we just go already?"

And so, with a compromise reached, we leave for the arena.

***

Now, I've been in thousand-seat arenas before, obviously. But, I have to say, being on this side of the glass is a different experience altogether. The girls and I sit next to Dr. Kirby, who insists that I call him Adrian when we meet outside of the hospital, and his wife, Grace.

Chuck had warned me beforehand that her mother is the Ultimate-Mother type. She wanted to have lots of kids but couldn't, for all sorts of reasons. So she took to "adopting" all of her daughter's friends, like Ava and her brother, and Dominik. She adopted Pierce for a completely different reason, since he's her unofficial son-in-law.

So I'm not too surprised when she hugs me as soon as she learns my name, and I try not to stiffen up. She insists that we sit down next to each other, and she asks me about my life. Not in a fan-girlish way, though she does admit that she's followed my career in the Seniors and that she admires me as an athlete, and not in a reporter way either. She asks in a way that says she really cares about me, even though it's the first time we've met. I've never had someone treat me this way, not once they knew who I was, until Ava and Grace, and Chuck.

The players are circling the ice, warming up. Ava claps softly, more for herself than for the players.

"Come on, bro. Get back in the game."

Chuck dryly asks: "you realize that you cheer for your brother more than for your boyfriend?"

"Dom is playing fine. My brother, however, is not in it because he's too distracted. You watched the same away game I did Tuesday, right?"

"He'll be fine, it's been a week, he's got to be over it, by now."

"I know how long it's been. I've been talking to him on the phone almost every day, and I'm telling you; Luke just hasn't been the same since airport girl stood him up!"

Wait, what?

"What are you talking about?"

"I'm talking about my brother and his failed date Monday night, Anna."

"Don't you remember, she's been talking about this all week?"

Chuck's sarcasm barely registers. I've got bigger worries right now. "What's that about an airport?"

"Didn't I say? It's where he met her. Saturday morning. He was coming home from an away game, and there she was."

Ava's brother met a girl at the airport Saturday morning. A girl he made a date with on Monday night, only she didn't show. Ava's brother is a hockey player. Ava's brother is called Luke.

At this moment, the giant screen shows one of the players of the Jets, with his name and number in subtitles. Number 17, Lucas Crawford.

It's him, all right.

Oh, crap.

***

I have to get my head back on right. It's just a girl. But seriously, I can't stop thinking about her. I have to, though, I really do. It's done, she's gone, it's over.

This is what my mind has been like all week. I'm always thinking about her, or telling myself that I shouldn't. I'm not sure how much longer I can take this: it's driving me nuts!

I really, really have to focus on this game. I did well enough on the away game Tuesday, but anyone who knows me knows I wasn't really all there. This shit can't go on anymore.

I'm on the ice, warming up, doing my thing. I look up to the section where I know Ava will be sitting with Chuck. I know that the doctor and missus Kirby will also be there, as will this new neighbor that Ava wants to set me up with.

I see Ava and Chuck. I see the doctor and his wife. I see a girl, sandwiched between them. She looks pretty small, and she has a lot of curly red hair. She's wearing a team t-shirt with a leather jacket, and a green hat and mittens.

Green hat and mittens. Just like the ones Anna wore.

It's just a coincidence, dude. There are lots of hats and mittens like that in the world. It's not even the right hair color.

But even as I think that, I keep on staring. The more I look, the more I'm convinced that it's her. Anna. But what would she be doing there? What are the odds? And am I just seeing her because I want to see her, or is it really her?

I spend the rest of warm up and the first period staring at her whenever I can, trying to reason with myself, to figure out what the hell is going on. After first period the guys corner me.

"Dude," Pierce says. "You're worse than Tuesday, man. What's the matter with you? Get your head back in the game!"

"Did you see the girl sitting with your girlfriends?" I ask.

"Who, Anna? Yeah, we saw her."

"She's the new neighbor, the one Ava wants to set you up with," adds Dom. "I know you know, because I overheard her telling you about it."

"The neighbor, her name's Anna?"

"Yeah, we just said it was." It was Pierce who answered, though Dom looked just as confused.

"And she moved in Saturday?"

"Yeah..."

"Did she have brown hair then?"

From the look on Dom's face he connected the dots. And that's all the confirmation I need.

Pierce, however, is still confused. "Yeah. How'd you know that?"

"Dude," I answer. "It's her. Anna. She's airport girl."

"No shit!" Pierce laughs so hard, he looks like he's getting belly cramps from it. It's time to head back for second period, but Dom holds me back for a sec. "I've heard she spent the whole day at the hospital Monday, with tests for her leg. Also, I don't think the way you've been playing so far will have impressed her."

Shit, he's right.

But wait, do I want to impress her? She's the one who didn't show up on Monday.

That's because she spent the whole day at the hospital, you dick.

But what happened to not wanting to impress her by being Lucas Crawford, superstar?

Screw that. I've got me a girl to get.

***

"Woo-Hoo! That's my brother! Look at him! He's on fire tonight!"

And so he is. After a pretty quiet first period, Luke comes out like someone lit a fire under his butt. He just scored his third goal.

Ava's going out of her mind with pride. And she really does cheer louder for her brother than her boyfriend. It's kind of funny.

The game ends with the Jets winning four to one. As people slowly file out of the stands, Adrian and Grace say their goodbyes, wishing us "young'uns" a good evening and reminding us not to drink and drive. Seriously. I've never heard someone actually say that to someone else. Ava reassures them that she's the designated driver for us ladies tonight, and the gentlemen are on their own, which is good enough for the Kirbys.

The moment of truth is looming. I feel like someone is doing macramé with my intestines but, at the same time, I just want it to be over.

We make our way through the arena to the locker room. And we wait. The players come out, some of them stop and say "hi"; you can tell that Ava and Chuck are regulars here. There are a few reporters waiting further up but, for the most part, the corridor's empty.

Then the boys come out. Dom, Pierce, and Luke. My boots suddenly become the most fascinating things in the universe. There's that spot of salt dirt, on my left boot, that looks like a fish. A kindergartner's version of a fish, but still.

"Luke!" I hear Ava call. I don't look up from the salt kindergartner fish on my left boot.

"Hey sis." I know that voice. It's him, all right. I already knew it was him, but there's something about hearing his voice that makes it even more real. "Chuck. Hi, Anna."

I hear female gasps and male chuckles. Great, he somehow figured it out and he told the boys. This is so embarrassing.

I feel a finger slide under my chin, and my face lifts.

"I like your hair like this," he says, smiling at me. He doesn't look mad. He looks happy, and... tender, and... Damn it, Luke. Don't look at me like that. I can't handle this right now.

But still I smile back. I can't help myself. "Thanks."

"Oh my God!" Ava squeals. She just figured it out. "You're airport girl!" Yep. She figured it out. "Well, since I know now why you stood my brother up on Monday, I forgive you. This is so perfect, really. It's like, fate pushing you together. Let's go out and celebrate!"

"I'm not hooking up with your brother tonight, Ava." Oh my God, did I really just say that out loud?

Everyone starts to laugh, so I'm pretty sure that I did. "Ooh, rejected!" Exclaims one of the boys, I think it's Pierce. I can't tell for sure because I'm hiding my face in my hands. I'm never looking any of these people in the eyes, ever again.

"Hey, she said not tonight," answers Luke. "Gives me hope for the future."

Oh, wonderful. Someone just kill me now.

The laughter sound like it's moving away from me. Good. Leave me here alone to die of embarrassment.

"Hey." Apparently, this isn't my lucky night. Luke is still there, and he's pulling my hands away from my face. "I'm sorry. I guess it's kind of a side effect of hanging around with boys, there's no taboo except our mothers and sisters. Like, Dom better not say anything about Ava in front of me and he knows it. I didn't mean to upset you."

"You didn't, really. I'm the one who opened my big mouth."

"It was a great reply, though. Perfect comedy timing. We should take this act on the road." I laugh, and he looks like he just won a huge prize, and it's not fair. "How about we start at Goodman's?"

I really shouldn't. I don't have the time or the space for this in my life right now.

But I nod anyway.

CHAPTER 5

Ava is jumping up and down with joy, at least metaphorically speaking. I'm half-expecting her to organize a slumber party when we get home Friday night, so she can gush about destiny and how great her brother is like they do in all those teen girly flicks. Maybe things like that don't happen in real life.

Or maybe she's just saving her energy to plan something else.

"Ice skating? You want me to go ice skating? Today?"

"Of course. There's a few local rinks that have open ice days on the weekend. I've called the boys, and I talked to Chuck, and everyone agreed."

"You didn't talk to me."

"I can't imagine that you would say no. Why wouldn't you want to go ice skating?"

Since my appointment with Doctor... I mean Adrian, I have come to terms with the idea that I'm going back on the ice. Mostly. But I thought that the first time I would be alone, so I could have a good freak out in private first. So no-one would be there to see if I fall, the way I did the last time. But having to skate in front of all these strangers? Or in front of my new friends? They know who I am, now. Won't they expect an Olympic performance out of me?

I grab the only excuse I can think of. "I don't want to go skating without my doctor's approval." It worked on my mother, to a degree, so it should work on anyone.

"Are you kidding me? Come on, Anna. It's just going around the rink in circles, and we're all going to be there. It's going to be fun. Please?"

While Ava begs, Chuck picks up her cell phone and fiddles with it. A few seconds later she says, "hey dad! Listen, we're planning to go skating, the whole gang. Can Anna come? You know, with her leg?"

I have to admit, right now, I really can't decide if I like Chuck or not.

She hands me the phone. "He wants to talk to you."

I pick up the phone. "Hello, Doctor Kirby." Not the hospital, but close enough.

"Hello Anna. So, planning to go skating, are we?"

"Maybe."

"Well, you're about at the stage where the athlete is encouraged to begin sports-related training again. So, assuming that you are careful; you know, go slowly, no sharp turns, no jumps, stop when you feel tired or if your leg starts to ache, I can't think of a reason why you shouldn't go."

I can, but I strongly suspect that the "for God's sake, don't force me to embarrass myself in front of my new best friends, their boyfriends and this really cute guy who spent all of last night flirting with me" argument isn't going to work.

"All right. Thank you, doctor."

We exchange our goodbyes. I hang up the phone and hand it back to Chuck. "I guess I'm going ice skating."

Ava squeals and jumps to hug me. Chuck is looking very pleased with herself. I try not to let my anxiety show.

***

I could kill my sister sometimes.

Ice skating? She wants us to go ice skating, all of us, with Anna? With Anna!? Susanna Miles, the Olympic silver

medalist and world champion figure skater, as she introduced herself last night. 'Everyone else knows, so I might as
well tell you myself,' she said.

It's not that I'm intimidated by her status or anything.
I won the Rookie of the Year, and I'm in line this year for
Best Scorer. But that's hockey. And besides, Anna hurt her-
self. Won't she be nervous at the idea of skating again?

But that's all done anyway. Ava said Anna agreed to
come. All I can do is keep an eye on her.

The girls all arrive together. We guys are there waiting
for them, skates on and ready to go. The girls each have
their own skates, and immediately begin lacing up. Ava is
the first done, and she grabs Dom's hand and races off,
almost sending a poor kid that happens to be in her way
tumbling down. Chuck was the next done, and she took off
with Pierce, rolling her eyes.

Subtle, sis. Subtle.

I look down at Anna. She is very careful in lacing her
skates. Very deliberate. Almost like she's stalling. All right,

then. I've got some time. I could go ahead and begin circling around, but Ava would have my head for leaving Anna alone. And, let's face it, I don't want to.

After a few moments she freezes and looks up. I smile at her.

"What?" She asks.

"What, what?"

"Why are you just standing there, looking at me?"

"It's a nice place, and a nice view."

"You can go ahead, you know. You don't have to wait for me."

"I want to."

"Why? So you can have first class seats to watch me fall?"

I knew it. She's nervous about skating again. Damn you, Ava. Why'd you have to push her?

"Anna, I'm not going to let you fall."

"You won't be able to stop it."

"Anna, please. Look at me," I say, showing off my six foot, two inches, 250 pounds frame. "And look at you," I say, waving a hand at her five foot, one inch, maybe 130 pounds body. "No offense, honey, but if I decide you don't fall, you don't fall."

She considers that for a few seconds, then she nods and gets up. She takes a few deep breaths, and slowly steps onto the ice in front of me. Her breathing is now very quick and shallow, and I'm afraid she's going to pass out if she keeps it up.

"Breathe, Anna. It's fine. You're doing fine. One step at a time."

We begin to glide in step. Even in the first slow and tentative steps, keeping the pace with her is not as frustrating as I might have imagined. She gains confidence, and with it rhythm. I look down to find her smiling ecstatically.

"Not bad," I tease. She squeals in response.

The instrumental track piping through the speakers fades out, and is replaced by 'Baby, It's Cold Outside'. I look around and find Ava talking to a rink employee. She catches my eye and smirks.

I'm forced to repeat myself. Subtle, sis. Very subtle.

Anna groans. "Urgh, that song!"

"What? What about it?"

"I just have a very low tolerance for this song. For one thing, there's the underlying skeeviness. Best case scenario, the girl plays coy and says no but really it's only so that the boy can chase her. Worst case scenario, it's basically date rape. Even if one overlooks that, it's so overplayed, like it's the only winter-themed love song."

Okay... That backfired. I bet Ava wasn't planning that reaction at all, which makes it even more satisfying.

"Well, it kind of is," I say, playing the devil's advocate.

"It is not. There's also 'Let It Snow'."

"What?"

"Come on! 'When we finally kiss goodnight, how I hate going out in the storm, but if you really hold me tight, all the way home I'll be warm. The fire is slowly dying, but my dear we're still good bye-ing, and as long as you love me so, let it snow.' It's all about a romance. And it can be sung by both a man and a woman, so no skeeviness."

"Yeah, I guess I see what you mean. Bet you can't name another one, though."

She stays silent just as the male singer croons 'man, your lips look delicious'. She's pursing her own lips in concentration. Delicious, indeed.

Slow down, man. You're not there yet.

"Not off the top of my head, no. But, 'Let It Snow' is the superior of the two."

"If you say so."

"Hey!" Pierce runs up to us. Great timing, there, buddy. "Anna's on the ice. That's great. Come on, show me something. Like a spin, or a fancy jump."

Chuck hits him in the shoulder, hard. The color drains from Anna's face and I'm getting ready to punch him myself, and not in the shoulder.

"I... I can't. My knee... The doctor said-"

"No, no, I meant show me!" says Pierce, thereby saving his nose from another break. "I've always wanted to do that stuff. Tell me how. I bet I can."

"Oh." Anna looks so incredibly relieved, she actually starts laughing. "You can't."

"Oh, come on! You don't know that."

"I do know that. You can't. Not today. See those?" She bends down to point at her skates. Shit! I can't be caught staring at her like that. The other side of the arena looks fascinating all of a sudden. "Those are called toe picks. Figure skates are designed with them, to allow the skater to stop and turn without the great wind up required by the speed skater, or the hockey player. Your skates are made for speed, and mine for agility. That's just the way it is."

Pierce pouts and mumbles "fine", before skating away.

"He's such a baby when he doesn't get his way," complains Chuck. She turns to face Anna, but I keep my eye on him. I don't like the look in his eyes, he's planning something. And sure enough, three seconds later, he's racing toward us. I just have the time to position myself in front of Anna and protect her from the shower of ice Pierce sends flying toward us, and the others around us.

"How that's for agility?" He yells.

"You idiot!" Chuck yells back. "Look at what you did, you baboon! You sent ice all over me!" She takes off her hat and begins hitting him with it, while he tries to apologize. I guide Anna safely away.

"Are they really, actually dating?" Anna asks me.

"Oh yeah. And they're like this all the time, too. Give them a minute or two and they'll start making out."

"Wow. You're kind of an amazing group of people to know."

She's totally including me in that. On purpose. That's great! Progress!

"Yeah, I guess," I answer, trying to sound modest. "You're a good addition to the group," I answer more honestly. She's so cute when she blushes.

***

I'm having a wonderful time. I try to be careful; at about three thirty, when my leg begins to ache, I go back to the bench. Luke comes with me, no questions or comments. We spend the rest of the afternoon talking about the skaters, about the gang. I learn that Adrian is the team doctor for the Jets; I guess it's one of the reasons he couldn't go to Toronto. A happy accident of fate, you could say.

Then, at about six, it all comes crashing down. I am in the arena bathroom when I overhear a group of girls walking in.

"Did you see Luke Crawford out there. OMG, he is so dreamy."

"Who's that girl he's with?"

"That's Susanna Miles. You know, the figure skater? She got silver at the Olympics."

"I heard she busted her knee and can't skate anymore."

"She was skating right then."

"That's not Olympic stuff. She probably can't compete anymore, and that's why she's dating Luke. A has-been who's clinging on to fame by dating someone famous, so pathetic."

Is that what I look like? Like some fame whore?

I don't care that Luke is some big shot hockey player. I care about my reputation, and it looks like being seen together makes us both look bad. I'm not even sure that I want to date him, for God's sake! Him or anyone, I'm just not ready to date. So why would I do this to myself?

Maybe I should just take a step back.

When the group goes out to dinner I make an effort to talk a little to everyone, not allowing the couples to pair off again. When we go for a walk after dinner I stick between the girls, once again avoiding the coupling off.

I try to be subtle, but I guess I fail.

"What are you doing?" Ava asks.

"What?" I try to play dumb. "You're the ones who invited me. I should spend some time with you two."

"We have plenty of time to spend together later. Luke spent all dinner trying to talk to you, and you ignored him. And now he's moping, and I hate to watch my brother moping. So stop it!"

Ava storms off. Chuck stays behind, thankfully.

"Is it because of what the girls in the arena bathroom said?"

Or maybe not so thankfully.

"How do you know that?"

"I was coming in as they were coming out. I heard. Tell me you don't actually believe what they said."

"They have a point."

"No, they don't. Or do you really think that girls only date hockey players for the celebrity factor? What about me and Pierce, or Ava and Dom?"

"It's not the same, Chuck."

"Why not? What's the difference?"

"The difference is that I'm a has-been, and you're a never-was."

"I beg your pardon?"

"You're the person no-one has ever heard of who ends up married to George Clooney. I'm like those actors who had a successful sitcom in the eighties, and then the sitcom ended, and they made some terrible B-movies, and now they are doing guest spots on Law and Order, or on Hollywood Squares, or some stupid reality show."

"That's not at all what you are."

"It's what I look like."

"Who cares about 'looks like'? You can't let what other people think decide what you should do with your life."

"I have to, Chuck. If I return to the competitive circuit, then I have to return to that mindset. Half-athlete, half-celebrity. I have a responsibility to the public, and an image to maintain."

Chuck looks like she would like to argue some more. I'm not sure why she doesn't.

"Maybe you're right," Chuck says after a while. "Maybe I don't understand how things work at your level of professional sportsmanship. You know who does? Luke. You should talk to him."

And she leaves. Dom and Pierce are nowhere to be found; I'm left alone with Luke. He looks so sad. I feel terrible.

"How much of that did you hear?"

"Most of it, I guess. At least, I got the part about you being the new Melissa Joan Hart."

I snort. It's a little funny. I wish it was funnier. I wish there was a way to make this work.

"I don't know, Luke. I don't know what to do about you. I like you a lot, but my life is such a mess right now. And maybe Chuck has a point: if I'm letting what other people are saying about me dictate my relationship, I guess that means I'm not ready to be in a relationship."

"You know what I think?" He replies. "I think we've both fallen victim to the Ava syndrome."

"The what?"

"The Ava syndrome. Now, I love my sister, but Ava has this habit of fixing other people's lives, of bossing them around until things work out the way she wants them to.

She wants us married with babies, so we're letting ourselves move faster than we otherwise might. I mean, we've only known each other two weeks. It's okay to take things a little slow."

"You really mean that?"

"Sure. You know what? Instead of putting all this pressure on ourselves, how about we agree that we are friends, that we enjoy each other's company, and agree to continue hanging out every once in a while, then see if we get in a better mindset for something else."

"I might not, you know. I might ever get to that mindset," I warn him.

"That's fine. I just want to spend time with you, as much as you'll allow. So," he pulls out his cell, "how about we start by exchanging phone numbers?"

He smiles at me, and I can't resist that look on his face. Let's hope he never figures it out, or I'll never win an argument. I pull out my own phone, feeling like I'm crossing the Rubicon.

CHAPTER 6

Luke keeps his promise. We keep things slow and he doesn't put me under any pressure. It's a busy time for him, as it turns out. He plays about four games a week, which is twice as many as usual. If I understood the explanation he gave me correctly, the reason is that the negotiations between the NHL and the players union took a long time to get settled, but the owners wanted to give season tickets holders their money's worth. Therefore the boys have to play the same amount of games, even though the season's now officially two weeks shorter. It's the kind of schedule the teams keep during Olympic years, like next year will be.

I wonder if it's harder to keep that kind of schedule two years in a row. I guess I'll see then. Assuming we're still together next year. If we're even together now. I honestly have no clue what is going on right now. Besides, I have other things to think about.

This is an especially difficult week for me. It's the Canadian National Championship week.

I've spent my daily phone calls with my mother listening to her bemoan my absence. How in this crucial pre-Olympic year, I could, nay, I should, be out there, securing my position. I'm not sure why she's freaking out so badly about the National. In 2009, she was all about the world championship. Making sure I finished high enough to go to the Olympics, and also low enough to make sure no-one else got sent.

I'm guessing that it's part of her ongoing campaign to make me feel bad about my injury, because the busted knee and the ruined season aren't bad enough. I should feel the deep-running shame for not having seen that patch of rough ice before I tried skating on it.

She's going to be texting me all night. I know because she said she would. She wants to make sure that I'm watching, that I'm taking notes on my "competition." I think about turning the phone off, but I don't want to risk missing a text from Luke.

He just sent me one right now. "Good luck tonight, wish I was there with you."

I wish you were here too. Stupid hockey game.

So, I'm all prepared for this evening with a large meat-lover's pizza. My mother would be furious if she knew. She hates junk food of any kind, and for all my life she watched my weight and nutrition like a hawk. Knowing this only makes the pizza more appealing. I understand that athletes have to keep a certain regimen, but I'm not back to training yet. I'll enjoy this while I can.

Just as I'm about to take the first bite, someone knocks on the door.

"Yeah?" I call out. Bad manners, I know, but what can I say? I don't want to move.

"Hand over the pizza and no one gets hurt."

What the hell? Ava? I walk up to the door and open it. Ava rushes in and jumps on the pizza, grabbing the first bite. Which is absolutely not fair! I paid for the thing, I should get to eat it first.

"There goes your diet," says Chuck as she walks in.

"It's exception day," answers Ava.

"Oh, right, the day ends with a Y. So, what are you doing, Anna?"

"I was going to watch the Nationals, and you're totally going to pay me back for that pizza."

"Why?"

"Because I paid for it, and I didn't even get to eat one bite before you jumped on it."

Ava has the decency to look sheepish at my comment. "Oh. Sorry. But I meant why are you watching the Nationals?"

"Because I should be there."

"Oh," says Chuck. "A pity party. We need alcohol. I'll be right back."

***

The alcohol, the pizza, my two best friends, and the texts from Luke made the whole evening a lot more pleasant that I had expected it to be. Even my mother wasn't as terrible as I thought she would be. Maybe she got engrossed in the competition and forgot about me.

According to her, my biggest concern should be this seventeen-year-old called Cicely Novak. She's blond and tan, probably fake on both sides, and she's my exact opposite, skating-wise. Her jumps are strong, but her transitions and her spins are awkward. Her choreography is... very mature, for her age. Almost risqué. Not something I would ever do. How am I supposed to watch out for someone I have nothing in common with?

But anyway, soon enough I am tipsy and sleepy from the overindulgence of pizza and other snacks that Chuck and Ava unearthed at their place and brought over. The Ladies Shorts were over, and we were just talking, lounging about.

"So, Anna, why won't you get together with my brother?"

I knew the evening was looking too much like a movie. I should have known this was coming. I should have seen it.

I hesitate before answering.

"Because I don't know how? Because I'm pretty sure that I'm not ready? All of the above?"

"What do you mean, you don't know how? Haven't you ever had a boyfriend?" Chuck asks.

"Of course not. A boyfriend would have been a distraction."

"Be serious. You don't really think like that, do you?"

"No, but my mother does. And I've been living with her all my life. She thinks reading a book or watching a movie is a distraction, she wasn't going to let me have a boyfriend."

"Well, you're not with your mother now," says Ava. "You can live your own life, and do the things that make you happy. Like date my brother. I think you're more ready than you think you are. You should see the way he looks at you. Like, we were together, the other day, and you texted him, and he got the goofiest smile on his face. You two should start dating, and get married and have babies. It would make me happy."

Ava, who had slid off from the sofa and was now sitting at my feet, leans over me, hugs my legs and rests her head on my knees.

"And, of course, Luke and I live to make you happy."

"Everyone lives to make everyone happy."

"Okay, she's had enough," declares Chuck. "Come on, Ava, let's get you to bed." She gets up and hoists her half-asleep roomie after her. "For the record," she adds, looking at me, "she's drunk but she's not wrong."

I watch the girls leave my apartment. I have no idea what Chuck means. Luke and I really live to make Ava happy?

I think about calling Luke. But then I remember the phrase "drunk dialing", for some reason. I seem to remember that it's bad. So instead, I stare at the phone until I fall asleep.

CHAPTER 7

On Wednesday morning we all get a text from Anna, "Got the official okay. Starting training today."

That text makes my day. Watching her get back on the ice for the first time since her injury, two weeks ago, had been one of the best things I ever saw. I want more of that. More of the ecstatic smile, the squealy, shaky laughter that grows stronger the more confidant she is. I want to see that again. And here's a perfect opportunity to do so, without having to share.

We just came back from two away games in two days and, thankfully, we're getting a bit of a break. Coach is giving us the day off. The girls are working, and the boys have plans, so it's me and Anna. I call Ava to learn which rink she'll be training in, and my sister confirms that Anna's mom/manager made arrangements to rent the ice for her sole use. She'll be there alone. I hope I'll be a pleasant surprise.

Turns out I was the first one surprised; Anna wasn't on the ice. Instead she was sitting on a bench, with her skates next to her.

"Hello!"

She turned toward me. "Luke! What are you doing here?"

"I was hoping you wouldn't mind a little company," I answer, showing her the skates I brought with me. "Question is, what are you doing? And why isn't what you're doing skating?"

"I'm thinking." She turns back toward the ice and says nothing else. After a moment, I sit down next to her.

"Wish I had a penny with me."

She smiles. "You know, they're about to eliminate the penny. They've already stopped making them, I think, and they're going to whittle them out of circulation. What's gonna happen to that saying then?"

"Maybe it'll go up to a nickel. About time the inflation caught up with the values of thoughts, you know." She laughs. "So, you spot me your thoughts, I'll give you a penny soon as I have one?"

"Nah, we'll call this a gift. I was remembering my childhood. I grew up here, did you know that?"

"I didn't."

"All my life I've been skating. I don't actually remember a time when I didn't skate. My mother probably put blades on my feet as soon as I could walk."

"Of course she did. This is the True North Strong and Free. What else are we going to put on our children's feet?"

"Good point. I won some of my first competitions here, in this rink, actually. I... I'm trying to figure out at which moment in my life I decided that I wanted to compete. I can't remember. Maybe I never did."

"You're choosing now."

"Am I? Let's face it, Luke, what are my options? I've never even been to high school. I got a GED somewhere along the road, but that doesn't exactly open up a lot of possibilities. The only reason my mother is paying for me staying here is because she thinks it'll lead to my competing again, to Olympic gold. If I don't go back again, she'll cut me off, and she's in charge of all the money. That's not really what I call a choice."

"Maybe not. And I'm guessing talking to your mom is out of the question?"

"Well, it's complicated. There are a lot of weird family dynamics in motion here. I'm not sure how to explain, and you probably wouldn't understand anyway."

My father's voice rings in my head. '*Mon gars, r'garde-lé, mon gars, c'est l'prochain Rocket!*' I know plenty about weird family dynamics, which means I know enough not to push.

"You might be right about that. You know what I know, though?"

"No, what?"

"I know that you were happy on the ice Saturday two weeks ago. You had a good time. You're not going to be competing tomorrow, anyway. So, I say, let's have a good time. Let's put those skates on your feet. I brought music."

With a roll of her pretty green eyes, she puts her blades on while I plug my iPod into the speakers. She laughs when 'Let It Snow' starts to play. We chase each other around on the ice. After a little more coaxing, she shows me a few moves. Nothing super fancy, some zigzags and criss-crosses and slow spins. Watching her, I begin to understand why they call it dancing.

She looks beautiful.

CHAPTER 8

On Monday morning I wake up to something I have not woken up to in a very long time: the sound of my alarm.

The days since Wednesday have been spent either at the physical therapist's, on the rink getting slowly reacquainted with the ice, or in my apartment, thinking. I thought about what the girls had said o Ladies Shorts night; not that we all live to make Ava happy, but that I could get myself ready for the life I want. Of course, there's the slight problem of trying to figure out how. And I also thought about my conversation with Lucas, how I don't feel like I'm choosing to compete.

Then I had a flash: those two things are connected. To get myself ready for the life I want, I have to start making my own choices. I have to get in control of my life. I'm twenty-two years old, for the love of God! Most people my age are pursuing advanced degrees, or they have careers. Ava and Chuck are both around my age, and they both have their own businesses. And what am I doing with my life? Yeah, I'm competing, because my mom is making me. And I have no post-Olympics plan.

That's what I need to change. I need to make some plans. I need to make decisions for myself. At some point, that means I'll need to stand up to my mother, but I'll worry about that when I get there.

So, do I want to skate? Yes. I enjoy myself on the ice. I think I'd forgotten how much I enjoy skating. Especially when I'm doing it with friends, and with this cute guy who might be my boyfriend, although I've never used the word. That's another decision for another time.

Now the next question is, do I want to compete? It's hard to say. I don't have this raging, burning desire to win all the prizes, and I don't feel like my life will have no value if I don't. I've seen people like that in the circuit; they're not fun to be around. I could decide not to compete, do something completely different and still be satisfied with my life, I think.

But on the other hand, if I don't compete I'll always hear my mother's voice in my head, calling me a lazy quitter. I'll always wonder if I could have done it, what might have happened. If I can't get back to competitive levels, that's fine. I'll live with that. But if I never even try... It doesn't sit well with me.

So I've made the decision: I'm competing. Because if I don't, I will be disappointing myself.

That feels good.

Now, about having some control over my life. After much consideration, I came up with a plan, saved on my computer and on my phone, with a hard copy printed out and stuck to my bedroom wall, where I can see it first thing in the morning.

It reads something like this:

1) Get control of my career.

- Get back into a routine

- Call Liam, make sure he'll come here once I get the OK

- Get the medical OK in April

- Find a way to deal with my mother

2) *Get control of my finances*

- Learn how to budget

- Get some spending money

- Convince my mother to give me control of my accounts

3) *Have a mature relationship with Lucas*

- Baby steps ??????

So, yeah, it's not perfect, but it's a start. It also involves a lot of things that are out of my control, like getting my medical OK, and dealing with my mother. But there's time for that. For now, I'm tackling the first point on my list, the easiest one. Which is why I'm waking up to the sound of my alarm.

***

For the rest of the week, and all the weeks for the foreseeable future, my schedule looks like this: I get up at 6:30. I eat breakfast. At 7:00, I head to the gym (there is one only two blocks away from the apartment building, it's on the small side but it does the job) for 90 minutes. I shower, change, go back to my apartment. At 10:00, on Mondays, Wednesdays and Fridays, I have my physical therapy appointments. The other mornings, I run errands. At 12:00, it's lunch time. At 13:00, I head out to the rink for three hours of training. As my knee gets stronger, I expect the time I will spend training will increase, especially once I don't have to go to p.t. anymore. The rest of my evenings, and my weekends, are free for now, so long as I'm in bed by 22:30. The schedule keeps up pretty well. For now, three hours of training is the maximum I can do, and I can't do much during that time, but I feel good.

I call Liam Thursday morning. Liam Daly is my coach. He's the coach I've been training with the longest; he came to the Olympics with me. I like him a lot, and it feels really good to hear from him. He gives me some tips for my training, some questions to ask Caleb that I hadn't thought about, and he promises to come to Winnipeg and check me out when I get the medical OK. So that went really well.

On Saturday morning, I visit Chuck and Ava, with my list. I figured they might help with the financial aspect.

Chuck's reaction is to delegate to Ava: "I don't know what I'd contribute to the conversation. She's the one who's good with money," she says before heading back to her room.

Ava, on the other hand, is all over this conversation. She has lots of reading suggestions and practical advice, the first being that I need to get the spending money before I learn to budget.

"Have you thought about getting a job?"

"Yeah, I have, but if I'm going to be serious about training, I won't have the time. I spend 15 hours a week on the ice, plus seven and a half hours a week at the gym, and that time will only go on increasing."

"Right. And most of the jobs you'll be getting, you'd be standing all the time; that can't be good for your leg. Maybe you could sell something? You must have stuff that could get you the kind of money we're talking about. Some collectible or whatever."

I don't like the idea of selling my mementos. It feels too sad, and a little crass as well, but I might not have a choice. "What kind of money are we talking about?"

"An average, middle class yearly income? About thirty thousand dollars, maybe."

What?! Oh, my God! I don't have anything worth that much money. Who would be crazy enough to spend that kind of money on some of my old junk anyway?

Unless...

"Hey, Chuck! I figured out a way you can contribute to the conversation." I wait until she walks back into the room. "How much do you think I could get for my car?"

By the end of the day, I had sold back my disgusting Mercedes SUV, bought a lovely second hand coupe to replace it, switched the lease on the apartment to my name, with a first and last month down payment, and I still had over eighty thousand dollars in my bank account. I have done, am doing, everything I could on my own. Now I have to wait for April, and find a way to deal with my mother. And with Lucas.

CHAPTER 9

Okay, this has gone on long enough. Things have to change, and I'm going to have to be the one who does the changing. I'm as ready as I'm ever going to be.

I'm going to ask Lucas Crawford out.

I want us to go out, on a real date. I want the romance. I blame all the stupid Valentine's Day ads that have been showing up all over the place for the last two weeks. I also blame Ava, who's been gushing about her elaborate plans with Dom. And while I'm there, I'm also going to blame Chuck, and the little smirk she had when she said her Valentine's Day plans were private.

I want private plans, and elaborate plans, and I want candlelight dinners and diamonds and the implication that there's going to be sex. I'm not sure about the actual sex, but I'll have to get to that point eventually, right? Anyway, right now I want at least one real date.

I like Luke. I like spending time with him. I like that he makes the detour to my chosen gym to work out with me every morning he's in town. I don't have any idea where this is leading, but I figure I have to find out sometime. And the best way to figure that out is to go on a first date. A real, official, first date.

But if Lucas wants to go out with me, he'll just ask, won't he?

Well, maybe not. Maybe he's waiting for me to ask. At least, if I ask, I'll have a definitive answer soon enough.

I have to find the best time to ask. The guys are coming back from an away game this morning, and the girls have asked me to accompany them to the airport to pick them up, so I know I'll see Luke today. But I can't ask him out in an airport. And I can't ask him out for a first date on Valentine's Day. That just sounds ridiculous.

I'll just go pick him up. We'll have a nice chat, maybe tease our coupled-up friends a little, and I'll ask him out tomorrow, or the day after. Or something.

The plane is delayed for just under an hour. We make our way to the luggage belt and wait for them there, because by now even I know that it's useless to wait for them at the gate; we'll just get crowded out by the journalists. The boys make their way to us, eventually. The couples pair off, and I'm left alone with Lucas.

"Hi."

"Hi."

"So, how did the game end yesterday?"

"You mean, you didn't watch until the end?"

"It went into overtime, and I have a very strict curfew."

"Ah, of course. Well, we lost."

"Oh, I'm sorry."

Luke shrugs. "It's not so bad. It's still worth a point. We've got two months until the playoffs, and we're in a decent position. If we can avoid screwing up in the next few weeks, I'd say our chances are good."

"Did you just give me the press brush off?" I pretend to be offended, although there's a little bit of truth in my question.

"No, because I can't say 'screw up' when I'm talking to the press. I don't want to jinx it with too much enthusiasm, but we have a good team, and we could go pretty far, maybe even all the way."

"That's great. So, I was thinking, maybe we could go out. Like, on a date."

What is going on with me?! I said I wasn't going to do that!

"Not tonight, because I realize that it would be awkward. You know, a first date on Valentine's Day. But soon. You know, if you want to, I mean."

Now, I stop talking. Why did it take me so long to stop talking? Why did I start talking about that in the first place? The damage is done, now. I have no idea how Luke is taking this crazy collection of sounds that just tumbled out of my mouth, pretending to be words, because I can't look at him. I've got my eyes trained on my boots, trying to erase the last minute or so out of reality.

"Anna?"

"Hmm?"

"How does Saturday sound?"

Wait, really? I look back up and find him smiling at me. My own smile is so sudden, and so enormous, it actually hurts my cheeks a little. "Really?"

He nods. "To be honest, I was beginning to think you were never going to ask."

***

Anna and I are going out. It's finally happening. Jesus Christ, I was going out of my mind waiting for her to make the next move. I talked myself in and out of asking her a dozen times. 'Don't rush her, let her set the pace.' 'Maybe she's too shy, if I don't say something she might think I don't like her.' All the time.

But anyway. It's done now, thank God, and it's Saturday night. I have a game tomorrow afternoon, so we agreed not to stay out too late. The plan is early dinner, and then I have a surprise for her. It's a gamble, but it's something that's important to me. If Anna and I are going to be a long term thing, she might as well know this right out of the gate. I'm not playing games this time. I had too much of that with Talia.

I get to her place, hoping she followed my advice and went with a nice but casual look. Since I'm wearing a checkered shirt and navy blue pants, if she wears a really nice dress one of us is gonna look pretty ridiculous. I'm pretty sure she's going to be fine, unless Ava got to her. My sister doesn't do casual. Ever. She owns one pair of jeans. They're designer, and white. I don't get that.

Anna opens the door wearing a pair of black pants, a button-down shirt with lots of different colored shapes on it and a green cami underneath. She looks great, and not fancy to the point of making one or both of us look ridiculous. I knew it would be fine.

"You look great," I tell her. Mostly because it's true, but also because I want to see her blush.

Dinner is nice. We're at a nice, basic steak house. I already knew she wasn't a vegetarian, and I didn't want to do fancy and fake, not tonight. I'm a guy who likes a good steak, and I'm not going to lie about it. She doesn't seem to mind.

The food is good, and so is the conversation once we agree not to talk about our families. I learn that her parents divorced when she was nine, that she's barely spoken to her father since, and that her mother/manager is a really touchy subject. As for my family, I answered the questions she asked about them, but she figured out soon enough that they're not exactly good conversation fodder, other than Ava. So we talk about other stuff, and dinner goes really well.

And then, it's time for the surprise.

"Bowling?" she asks, when we arrive at our destination. "You're taking me bowling?"

"Sure! Bowling is a great date activity. It's loads of fun. Plus, it's a kind of religion in my family. My father, my uncles, my grand-father, my great-uncles, they all played, mostly with each other. One of my uncle actually won silver at the National Championship in 89."

Anna smiles at me, indulgently. "What?" I ask.

"Nothing. It's just... it's the most you've said about your family all night. It's okay," she adds quickly, probably in reaction to my expression, because I feel like crap right about now. I made her feel bad. "I get it, I really do. It's just nice to know that not all the memories are bad." She smiles sheepishly and I return the smile the best I can, because I want her to remember a nice evening. "So," she eventually says. "Bowling. I've never been before. I'll probably suck."

"That's okay. I haven't played in ages, I'll probably suck more than you do."

And we do both suck, although I suck a little less than her, according to the scores. I tried to throw the game, but she wouldn't let me.

After the game, it's time to go home. And it's time to answer the most important question: kiss her or not kiss her? I already know I'm not going to go full French on her, and I'm definitively not getting in her apartment, or in her pants, tonight. But I should probably do something.

Maybe a peck on the lips, or on the cheek. Maybe just a hug. This is so weird. Now I remember why I hate first dates so much.

We're back at her apartment. The moment of truth.

I think just a peck on the lips. A quick brush and then good night. I can do that.

I lean in. Our foreheads are pressed together. I rub my nose against hers.

And then she makes that sound. A sort of whimper, but not like she's scared. More like a high pitched moan.

Fuck. I can't do this. I say goodbye and run away. I'm such a loser.

CHAPTER 10

"I can't believe it. I thought my brother had game. This is so disappointing."

This is basically all I've heard from Ava since my date with Luke. How she can't bear to live with the idea that her brother and I didn't kiss on our first date.

I'm not saying I'm not disappointed, but I think she's making it bigger than it is. It's not like one of us is about to have their lips surgically removed and we'll never have the opportunity to kiss again.

"But it's been over a week already," complains Ava when I raise that very logical point.

"Yeah, and he spent most of that time on the road, with the rest of the team, which you already know."

"Whatever. They're home now, they don't have a game, we're going to Goodman's tonight, and I better see some action, or else."

"Oh, yeah, I want my first kiss to be in front of all you guys," I answer with a heavy dose of sarcasm, making her roll her eyes at me.

***

And indeed, there's no kissing at Goodman's that night. Not between Luke and I anyway. Ava and Dominik do plenty of kissing, as do Chuck and Pierce. Luke and I just do our best to ignore them when they get started. We joke around, make bets on who will take a break for oxygen first, or we start our own conversations or play little games, waiting for our friends to pay attention to us again.

"So," says Chuck during one of those breaks. "I saw the posters. March 3rd, isn't it?"

Pierce shivers violently, to the great amusement of Dominik, Ava and Chuck. Even Luke's smiling, but he's also tense.

"What's March 3rd?"

"The Polar Bear Plunge," answers Chuck.

"You mean, that thing where people jump in freezing water?"

"Right. There's a plunge being organized on March 3rd, to raise funds for the Paralympic committee. The whole team signed up to participate, in a show of support for their fellow athletes."

"Can't I support my fellow athletes by sending a check?" complains Pierce. "I'm a good ol' southern boy. I don't like the cold."

"You're not in the cold for long, you big baby. Besides, I signed up to jump with you guys. Just think, me in a bathing suit. You're going to need that cold water."

It looks like Chuck's comments have a positive effect on Pierce. "Not too cold, though. We wouldn't want to damage the equipment."

"Your equipment can handle it."

And they're off again. Ava rolls her eyes at them. "Get a room, guys."

I snort at her, while Luke says: "You're one to talk, sis."

"We're not that bad," Ava tries to defend herself.

"Yes, you are," Luke and I answer at the same time. But while I meant to be teasing, Luke appears to be a lot more tense. "Are you all right?" I ask him.

"Yeah, I'm fine. It's just... the jump..."

His voice trails off. I try to guess at the rest of the sentence. "You don't like the cold?"

"Oh, please," scoffs Ava. "We've jumped in colder water than that! Remember that time when we-"

"Yes, Ava," interrupts Luke. "I remember."

They spend the next several minutes staring at each other. I'd heard of people having conversations without words before, but it's the first time I've actually seen it happen. It's kind of fascinating.

I think Ava just lost whatever argument they seem to be having, judging by her eye-rolling. "Well, I'm going to get another round of drinks," she says, and gets up to do exactly that. Dominik raises an eyebrow and follows after her. Luke sighs and pinches his nose. He looks really tired.

"Bad memories?" I ask timidly.

121

"It's not that the memories are bad, it's just... it hurts, because you know the moments are never coming back. You know what I'm saying?"

Vague memories flutter through my mind; my mother, my father and I, a happy family. I'm not even sure if those are real, or if I made them up to give myself the illusion of a normal childhood. "Yeah, I know." Silence. For a long time, silence. "So, anyone can sign up for that Polar Bear Plunge thing?"

"Pretty much, yeah. Why, do you want to do it?"

Want is an exaggeration. A very big exaggeration. But it feels like the right thing to do, for some reason. "Well," I answer slowly. "I am an Olympian. I should support my fellow athletes. And it sounds like the sort of thing one should do once in their lifetime. A story to tell, so to speak."

"You're serious. You're really going to do this?" The sudden spark in his eyes, the huge smile on his face, they all convince me I'm making the right choice. I nod. How bad can it be, really?

***

What am I doing here, on a Friday afternoon, measuring bookcases and couches for my sister? She has a boyfriend, for the love of God! Can't he measure her furniture?

"Well, that's not going to go through the door, unless it's disassembled," I say, pulling my measuring tape back.

"Yeah, I know. Dom already measured," she answers, making the whole endeavor even more useless. "I really just wanted to ask you something."

"Since when do you need pretexts to ask me anything? Just spit it out."

"When was the last time you heard from mom?"

Wow. Did that question ever come out of left field! I'm about to say something when I realize I don't have an answer. I need to think about it for a while.

"I don't know," I finally say. "Two, three years, maybe. Since I told them both I was signing up with the Jets. What about you?"

"I haven't talked to mom since the day I left home. Do you think something happened to her? Maybe that's why dad is weird?"

"If something had happened, why not just tell us? We're not little kids. Besides, three years?"

"I know. I just want to understand-"

"There's nothing to understand, Ava. Sometimes these things just happen. Why do you make such a big deal out of it?"

"Because I want you to be happy, and I know you're not happy not talking to dad. Maybe if you just talked to him -"

"I'm leaving now. Goodbye, Ava."

Well, that was a pleasant five minutes. I need something to cheer me up.

I wonder if Anna's home.

I walk to her apartment and knock on her door.

"Just a minute! Mom, I need to go, there's someone at the door... What do you mean, new coach? I already talked to Liam... He doesn't coddle me, mom... Blaise Darrow? Who is that guy? I've never heard of him... You want me to begin training with a new coach, after an injury, during an Olympic season? I've been with Liam for five years, we have a good rhythm... It's my career, mom, I'm the one doing the skating, I should take an interest... But... You don't... Fine, fine, I'll talk to your guy, but Liam stays my coach on record. I really have to go. Bye mom."

A second later, she opens the door. "Oh! Hi."

"Hi."

"So... how much did you hear?"

"Hard to say, but I'm guessing pretty much everything after 'What do you mean new coach'".

"Oh." She pushes the door open and walks away. I take that as an invitation and follow her into the kitchen. I sit down next to her, waiting for her to start speaking.

"It's just... She doesn't listen to me. It's like talking to a wall. I always end up giving her what she wants. I feel so pathetic."

"I realize it's none of my business, but have you considered changing managers?"

"I can't."

"Why not?"

"She's my mom."

"She'll still be your mom, even if she's not your manager anymore."

"I think you're wrong," she says, and she looks so sad. "I don't like admitting it, and I hope I'm wrong, but I think that if I fire her I'll never see her again."

I wrap my arms around her, trying to give her some comfort. My poor, sweet girl. We have so much more in common than you think.

***

I feel a little better after talking to Lucas, although the whole new coach situation is still worrisome. I try to put it out of my mind, though, because I have other concerns right now: I'm about to jump into a barely thawed lake.

"Are you ready?" Luke asks. I'm not, but it's not like I have a choice now; we're the next group to jump. Pierce, at least, looks about as enthusiastic as I feel.

And then it's time, and we jump. It's... freaking cold, which I did expect, but also exhilarating, which I did not. We're out almost as soon as we're in, thank God, and we rush to the blankets. Luke is laughing, and he looks so handsome, I just feel this urge to kiss him. So I do.

I'm freezing, and I have to stand on my tiptoes to reach his mouth, and he wraps his arms around me, and it feels amazing. I'm brought back to reality by the catcalls of our friends. So much for not having my first kiss with Luke in front of them!

Chapter 11

Last Saturday's kiss turns out to be a lot more public than I could have ever imagined. Social media platforms are now flooded with pictures of the two of us, and the speculation is running wild. I expected my mother to have some sort of reaction, of the negative variety, but she remains silent on the subject during our phone calls. Mostly, she keeps on insisting that I try to move the date of my appointment with Adrian. She really wants me to meet that new coach. I don't like this. I don't like how fixated she is on that point. Something's going on, but I don't know what, and it's freaking me out.

There's nothing I can do about it now, though. I'm not going to get that appointment until April, so anything that has to happen will have to wait until next month.

The Sunday after the Polar Bear Plunge, Adrian and Grace invite us to brunch at their house. 'Brunch' turned out to be code for 'spend the whole day in their beautiful house, lounging around and eating too much food'. Another new experience. I love it.

Right now, the six of us are playing a game that Chuck dug out of her parents' game room. "Okay, okay, next question: which among you is the most likely to have a tattoo?"

"Come on, Chuck!" I protest. "Couldn't you have skipped that one? We all saw each other in bathing suits. We all saw Pierce's tattoo." Pierce has a giant eagle drawn on his left shoulder.

"But the question was: who is most likely to have a tattoo? It could be out of character for him."

"Please. He's a big, brawny show-off. He's exactly the type to have a tattoo."

"Okay, then. Flip side, who is least likely to have a tattoo?"

The whole group answers with my name, all at the same time. I roll my eyes, and hide my smile by taking a sip of orange juice. Let them think what they want. I turn my head and see Adrian leaning on the door jamb.

Damn it! I have to do it. I know the answer, but I have to do it anyway.

"I'll be right back." Luke begins to complain to his friends about chasing his girlfriend away while I walk up to the doctor.

"Hi."

"Hello, Anna. Is something the matter?"

"Not exactly. It's just, I have to talk to you. I promised my mother I would. She's been calling every day, asking about my appointment in April."

"I suspected as much. She's also been calling the office, asking for updates on your health. I haven't told her anything; doctor-patient privilege is sacred."

"Okay. But anyway, when she calls next, I'll be able to tell her I asked. That should satisfy her."

"I hope so, for your sake."

"Excuse me?" Where did that come from?

"Sorry, I know it's not my place to comment on these things. But I have to ask: how... comfortable are you with your mother's managerial style?"

I stare at him, trying to figure out what he's trying to say. "I'm not sure I understand your question."

"What I mean is that, during our conversation, she made some... comments, and, well..."

Oh, God, this is so embarrassing. Mom talked me down to my new doctor. I don't think it had the result she expected, but this is still so humiliating.

I try to play it cool, though. "Oh, okay. Well, I think she's been a little stressed lately. The season is ending, and since I couldn't compete, it affects my ranking, and so on. She's anxious to see me back on the ice, I guess. Once I'm back to full-time training, she should simmer down."

"I see. Well, she is your mother, you must know her best." I can tell that what he wants to say is 'I hope so for your sake' again. I appreciate his restraint. "When she calls back, you may tell her that your appointment is fixed, and that I refuse to move it forward."

I thank him. He pats my shoulder and walks away. That is when I notice Grace standing in the corner.

"Would you care to walk with me?" She asks. She takes me on a tour of the house. We don't talk much at first. I know she overheard enough of my conversation with her husband to make whatever talk we're about to have awkward.

"I don't have the easiest relationship with my mother," she eventually begins. "In fact, I don't have any relationship with my mother nowadays. She has some very old-fashioned ideas about the position of women in society. Being of a certain rank, her highest ambition was to make a good marriage, be the perfect housewife, and raise children who would fit in that mold; successful men if they were sons, perfect housewives if they were daughters.

"I was an only child, which was disappointing enough to begin with, but I enjoyed pretty things and dressing well and having tea with my friends. I even insisted on having a real tea party every year for my birthday until I was fifteen, so my mother was satisfied in that, at least. It all changed when I told her that I wanted to become a lawyer. She declared that no daughter of hers would ever have a profession, especially not a man's profession, which she considered the law to be. My father was no help; he paid for my education but told me not to upset my mother.

"I tried to compromise; I studied to become a paralegal instead. It felt humiliating to me, becoming a glorified secretary instead of what I really wanted, but I thought it would please her. It did not. The day I graduated I was offered a job, and she promised me that if I took that job she would never speak to me again. I did, and she did. She didn't even come to my wedding with Adrian. The irony is, the firm I was working for went under just as Adrian's practice was starting to pick up, and just as I found out I was pregnant with Charlotte. So, I ended up being the housewife she wanted me to be, a doctor's wife to boot, but she never knew."

We stand in silence for a minute. "Grace," I finally say, "why did you tell me all this?"

"I wanted you to see that I understand something of your situation, and if you need someone to talk to, I am here."

* * *

A few days later, I have another unexpected conversation. It begins with my phone ringing, the caller ID showing an unknown number.

"Yes, hello? Who is this?"

"Um, Suzie?"

There's only one person in the world who calls me Suzie.

"Dad? Hi. I didn't recognize your number, is it new? Wait, where did you get my number?"

"I... well... I looked it up. I wanted to talk to you. I moved into a new place, but that was a while ago. I didn't think..."

My number is red listed, but then again, Dad is a policeman and he would have the resources to look it up. I'm surprised he'd make the effort, or risk his job like this. He never has before.

"Okay. So... how are you?"

"I'm good, thank you. How are you? I heard about your knee."

"Oh, that. Yeah, I'm getting better."

"That's good, that's good. So I was watching the game the other day, and they zoomed the camera in on you. Said you were dating one of the players."

"Yeah. So?"

"So... how is that going?"

"It's going well. He's a good guy."

"That's good. That's good."

"Since when do you follow the Jets, anyway?"

"I wasn't. It was a game against Washington. You know my friend, Bobby Stark? His boy Owen plays for Washington."

"Oh, I see."

"So... how's your mother?"

"Mom is, well, you know, mom. We're having some arguments these days, about a new coach she wants to hire. I don't think it's a good idea, but, well, she handles the money, so-"

"She what?"

"You know what, it's not even... let's just forget it, okay? I have to go. It was nice talking to you. Maybe I'll call you sometime, okay?"

"Sure, honey, anytime."

What the hell was all that about?

***

On Friday, April 5th, I have my appointment with Dr. Kirby. This is it. I can't imagine that he would have anything but good news to give me. Caleb has promised that my knee looks perfect, I've slowly been increasing my training, and my leg only feels stronger every day.

When Dr. Kirby gives me the official thumbs up I feel some relief, but mostly I feel determined. Now is the time to spring into action. Let's do this thing.

I call my mom and leave her a message. That's weird. She knew my appointment was today, she griped enough about it. I expected her to be sitting on the phone, ready to pounce the minute it rang. I also leave a message with Liam, and then I call everyone. The boys are at an away game, but they send their congratulations and their promises to do something the night after they come back. The night of their return, they have a game. The girls cook me a celebratory dinner.

I spend Monday evening with Ava and Chuck. We have a double-feature movie night about figure skating, "in my honor," says Ava. We watch some old movie about a figure skater and a hockey player who team up and fall in love, followed by an even older movie about another figure skater who returns to the ice after an injury leaves her blind. Not exactly the most subtle choices, but I still have a good time.

At ten o'clock, I say my goodbyes and go back to my apartment. I jump back when I see who is waiting for me at the door.

"Mother!?"

CHAPTER 12

"What are you doing here?"

"I've come to put your career back on track. It appears that you can't be trusted to do it. Aren't going to let me in?"

"Anna, I just remembered that I wanted to tell you..." Ava stops short, halfway down the stairs, when she sees that I'm not alone. "Oh, hello."

"Mom, this is my friend, Ava Crawford. This is my mother, Olivia Miles."

Ava extends her hand, which mom promptly ignores. "Well, Susanna? Let's get moving. I have been waiting almost half an hour for you, and we have much to discuss."

I turn to face Ava. "Sorry. I'll call you tomorrow, okay?"

"Are you sure you're all right?"

"Yeah, everything's fine. I'll call you."

"Okay. Bye."

I wait until she is well up the stairs before I finally open the door of my apartment to my mother. For some reason I don't like her being here, in my space, among my things. It's like she's trying to take over.

"I was surprised you didn't call me back on Friday," I say hesitantly, unsure how to begin this conversation.

"I had to make arrangements for my move here."

"That's another surprise; you said you'd never come back."

"Desperate times call for desperate measures. Clearly you need to be monitored. What have you done in the last four months except lounge around and bad-mouth me?"

Not this again.

"I have been training, more and more every day, and going to physiotherapy, and what do you mean, bad-mouth you? I never bad-mouthed you."

"Your father called me, Susanna. He told me about your conversation. He has better things to do than listen to you complain about me. Where did you get the idea that this would even work? You're old enough, you should know better."

What? Dad said that? But... he called me. I don't understand.

"In any case," she continues, "I will remain here until you return to Toronto, where we both belong."

"Where are you staying? Because I don't really have the... well, I guess I could always..."

"Please! What did you think, that I would sleep on your couch? I took a room at the Fairmont."

Five-star hotel, of course.

"I expect you to meet Blaise and I at the restaurant tomorrow morning. Eight thirty. We have a lot to discuss."

"Shouldn't we wait for Liam?"

"Why would we do that?"

"Because he's still my coach. We agreed."

"We agreed that you would meet Blaise."

"As long as Liam remained my coach on record! Mother, if you tell me that you fired Liam, that you lied to me like that, I'm quitting, right here and right now."

"You're not serious."

"Watch me!"

Something about the look on my face must have convinced her of how serious I was.

"You are being childish, and over-dramatic. Liam isn't here because I wanted you to give Blaise a fair chance. I didn't want you ignoring him and his input, and I knew that was what would happen if Liam came along. Two weeks, Susanna. That's all I ask. Two weeks of working with him, really working with him, not crossing your arms and pouting. If by then it's clear that things aren't working out, we'll consider other options."

It sounds logical. It's probably true that if Liam was there, I would turn to him. I probably would pay less attention to the new guy, especially since I've worked with Liam for five years and I've never even heard of this Blaise. I can give him a fair trial. Two weeks isn't too much to ask. And at the end, Liam will come and everything will work out fine. I nod.

"Good. Until tomorrow, then."

And, with those words, my mother leaves. I crumble on the couch, exhausted. More and more, talking to my mother feels like a boxing match. At least this time I managed to stick to my point, to make myself heard. So why do I have the feeling that she won the first round?

***

The next morning, after a fitful sleep, a slightly shorter-than-usual workout, and a crisis over what to wear, I arrive at The Velvet Glove, the very high-class restaurant of the

Fairmont hotel. I sit down in front of my mother almost exactly at eight-thirty. My display of punctuality is met with little more than a raised eyebrow. My tardiness, if I had been tardy, would have resulted in a lecture on my lack of respect.

She makes the introductions between myself and the man sitting next to her: I am her daughter Susanna, he, rather unsurprisingly, is Blaise Darrow, who will be coaching me for the time being. He gives her a weird look when he hears that; I guess my mother didn't tell him about the two week trial period. He must think that he'll be coaching me for longer than that. One of us is wrong.

I immediately dislike him. His smile is too big, too cheeky. The way he looks at me makes my skin crawl. It's like he's trying to turn his breathing into innuendo. It's disgusting, not to mention super-inappropriate.

I promised Mom I would give him two weeks, and I will, but he's getting the boot after that.

The waiter arrives soon afterward to take our orders. Blaise orders first, then mom. I start to order the omelet, when mom interrupts me. "Don't be ridiculous, Susanna. She'll take the plain yogurt, with a side of fruits. Nothing but water to drink."

"Excuse me. I'm an adult, fully capable of ordering for myself. I'll have the omelet and a glass of orange juice."

"I'm the one paying the bill, and the tip. She'll take the yogurt."

Apparently that's all the waiter needs to hear, because he walks away. "Mother. I think I'm the best judge of what I need to eat. I just did a full workout, and I'm about to do another one. I could use the calories."

"You look like you've already indulged in too many eggs."

"And just what exactly does that mean?"

"You're not so dense, Susanna. Don't pretend to be. I'm saying this for your own good, you know. You're the one who has to carry all that extra weight on the ice."

"I've lost five pounds since the last time you saw me."

That shuts her up, for about thirty seconds.

"Oh. Well, it's impossible to tell with that dress you're wearing. You should be careful to dress better; you are a public figure, and as such you have an image to maintain."

I'm wearing a dress I bought with Ava, one I thought was really cute and looked good on me. Before I can say anything else, though, Blaise speaks up.

"Don't be so hard on the kid, she looks great."

Ugh! The way he said that. It's some kind of gift this guy has, take a relatively general, seemingly harmless compliment and turn it into the motto of creep city. Judging from my mother's face, she doesn't like his tone either. Good. I might not have to fight too hard to get Blaise Darrow, super-creep, out on his ass at the end of his two week trial.

"Just lay off the omelets," she tells me abruptly. For the rest of the meal, mom and Blaise mostly ignore me to discuss their plans for the upcoming season. I follow along as best I can, but I'm having a harder time than I feel I should. A lot of it seems to be about the side stuff, the publicity, getting my name back out there. I think it's a bit early, considering Blaise has never seen me skate. Besides, my name is out there plenty. During the Nationals, the commentators brought up my name at least a dozen times. I try to point that out but they both repeat, in their unique tones, not to worry myself about it and to focus on my performance. I'm getting really tired of that. I'm getting really tired of this meeting. What am I even doing here?

"You know what? I think I left my leg warmers at the apartment. I'll meet you at the rink."

And I make my escape.

***

After a long, hard day on the ice, I come to several conclusions.

The first is that, no matter what else happens, at the end of these two weeks Blaise will not be my coach. I am quite ready to quit skating, if it comes to that. He is horrible.

The fake sweet and uber creepy demeanor of breakfast was replaced by a tyrannical attention to imaginary details. He had nothing but criticism for me; I couldn't do anything right. He made me run drill after drill, calling me every variation of stupid in the thesaurus.

That being said, my quitting might be the only way I'll ever be rid of him. As I was running drill after drill I watched the way he and my mom were acting with each other, and something became really obvious: they are sleeping together. My mother hired her lover to be my coach.

Or she hired me a new coach and then seduced him. I can't tell. I'm not sure which one is worse.

CHAPTER 13

The next day, I find a surprise waiting for me at the arena.

"Susanna, this is Julia Nebar," my mother introduces, although of course I already know who she is. She's a choreographer, and a fairly well known one at that. She has a very distinctive style; extremely energetic, strong Latin influence, passionate and sensual. Her routines are very good, and popular, and they tend to reach a lot of points when well executed. On the other hand, it is very easy to crash and burn on them. Besides, it's very much not my style; it relies heavily on all my weaknesses.

"Julia will be working with us. She's only in town for three days, so we have a lot of work to do and very little time to do it. I expect you to contribute."

"Of course, mother."

"That means you'll stay as late as Julia needs you to."

"Well... I have plans, for tomorrow night. I need to leave at seven."

"No, what you need to do is cancel."

"It's Luke's last home game of the season. I made plans with my friends to go see it a really long time ago. Surely, we can finish at seven one night. It's about the time you end for dinner anyway. I'll work later tonight and Friday."

"You'll work later tonight, and Friday, and tomorrow as well. Julia is only in town for 72 hours, and you will spend every single hour you possibly can working with her. Period."

"But..."

Blaise starts yelling. "Are you done with your whining already? Get your ass on the ice, now!"

This practice is especially difficult. My mind is not on the choreography I'm supposed to be learning, it's on the phone call I will be making tonight. I want to go to that game. It's a special game, and we're going out to celebrate afterward, the six of us.

My mom and Blaise keep me in the rink until eight o'clock that night. I'm pretty sure they just wanted to prove a point.

After the very long, difficult day, I go to the locker room to change. My mother catches up with me there.

"What do you want?" I ask her.

"I want to know why you're letting those people mess up with your game."

"What?"

"You were terrible today, and I think we both know why. You weren't thinking about your skating, you were thinking that your little friends would be disappointed in you. Why are you letting them influence you like that? Do you really think they care about you? You're like a toy to them, the celebrity, the Olympian. Right now, they get to show you around and talk about you and it makes them look important around other people. But once you start to really work, instead of just playing at it like you've done for six months, once you can't go out and party or have sleep-overs anymore, once you're on the road ten months out of the year, they'll get bored. They'll stop calling you, they won't want to spend time with you. As for that little boyfriend of yours, you appeal to him right now, with your shyness and your virginal aura. But he'll get bored, too, when he doesn't get any. He'll dump you and start seeing the puck bunnies who give it up in bar bathrooms again. I'm saying this for you, Susanna. They don't care about you. You need to focus on your skating, because in the end, it's all you have."

"You don't know them, and you don't know me. How dare you? Why are you doing this? Why would you say all that? Why is it so terrible for me to want to have a life out of the arena? Off the ice? My career won't last forever, you know. Why can't I plan for after?"

"Because after is bleak. One day, you'll look back on your career, on the best years of your life, and you'll hate

155

yourself because you let yourself get distracted and didn't do all you could have done. I'm saying this because you need to hear it, even if you don't like it."

I run out of the locker room, out of the arena, trying to forget the words of my mother. Ava and Chuck are my friends. They care about me. Luke cares about me. They aren't going to give up on me. Luke is a professional hockey player, for God's sake. Chuck and Ava are both dating professional hockey players. They know about the demands of the sports world. They won't give up on me because I've started training again. I know they won't.

Once I get home, I don't even have the energy to climb up the stairs. I just pick up the phone.

"Hello?"

"Ava, it's me, Anna."

"Hey, what's up?"

"I won't be able to come tomorrow."

"What? Why not?"

"My mother found a new choreographer. She's only in town for three days. I have to spend all the time I can in the rink with her, so we can work. You know, make the best of the time we have."

"But it's an evening game! Surely, you'll be finished by seven? We can pick you up right from the arena. It's okay if we're just a little late."

"I just finished, right now, tonight. I'll probably work as long tomorrow, and the day after for that matter. Things are getting serious, now. I'm back to full competitive training. I have a lot of work to catch up on for the next season."

"But it's not healthy for you to always keep working. It's just one night. Come on."

My mother's words are buzzing in my ears. Once they find out what it's really like for you, they won't want to play with you anymore.

"You know what, Ava? I can't really take a day off. I've just taken six months off, and those were six months that I couldn't afford to take off. This is my life now. If you can't deal with it, that's fine. I'll see you around. Or not. Whatever!" And I hang up the phone.

The next day's practice is especially rueful. I do my best to make up for my lack of attention of yesterday, and I guess I must have succeeded, because my mother doesn't corner me at the end of the session.

Much later that night, Ava knocks on my door. "Hey." she says when I open the door. "I just wanted to make sure that we were okay. I'm sorry about last night. I shouldn't have pushed so hard."

"It's fine."

"Are you sure you're okay?"

"Yeah, I'm fine. I'm just tired. It's been a long day. We're cool, okay? I just need some sleep."

But it's not that. Or not only that, anyway. I can't help myself. I'm leaving Ava before she leaves me.

CHAPTER 14

Ava warned me that Anna has been weird since her mother came into town. Since 'Weird' is one of the worst, least precise descriptors ever, I ask for more details, but she only answers: "you'll see when you see her."

Well, it's Sunday. The regular season is over, and I'm spending the day with Anna at her place. She is, well, weird. She's really quiet. She jumps up whenever I speak. She looks like she needs like 14 hours of sleep and then a greasy burger. She also looks like she's about to start crying, though God knows why. She's apologized three times for missing the game on Thursday, even though I keep telling her it's no big deal. We're making the play-offs, so there'll be other home ice games, and soon too.

And now, she's just been staring at me for the last five minutes. It's getting a little unnerving.

I'm about to ask what her deal is when she starts kissing me. Well, okay then.

It doesn't take too long to figure out that something is wrong with the kiss. She's way too tense, and she's breathing too fast. I pull back, and she's whispering "I can do this. I can do this."

"I know you can, but do you want to?"

She looks at me, shocked. "Don't you want to?"

That's a trick question, right?

Although, as I'm looking at her, I find a surprising answer. "Well, the deer caught in the headlights look you're sporting right now is kind of a turn off," I say truthfully. "What is going on? Was it something I did, or something I said? 'Cause if I made you feel pressured, well, I really didn't mean to, and I'm sorry." Sorry is a weak word; I feel like a huge asshole right now. I scared my girlfriend.

"No, no, you didn't. I was pressuring myself. I'm sorry. It's just... I don't want to lose you."

"You're not losing me! Where the hell did that come from? What is going on here?"

Instead of answering me, she starts to cry. Great! Huge asshole, take two.

"All right, all right. Let's try something else, okay? Let's just lie down," I lie back, waiting for her to do the same, "put your head on my shoulder, close your eyes, deep breath."

I hear her breath in, then out. "Now what?" she asks.

"Shhh. No talking during nap time."

She laughs, and I laugh too, but I'm serious. It's not fourteen hours and a greasy burger, but it's a start, and it's what she needs right now. I have no idea what's going on with her, other than it probably has something to do with her mom. I'm afraid of what's going to happen next week, when I'm on the road for the play-offs.

***

It's Wednesday. Theoretically there are only five days left in creepy Blaise's trial period, but I'm less and less sure that my mom will keep her word. She'll just harp on and on about how he's wonderful, and I'm an ingrate, and she'll never bring Liam back and I'll be stuck with creepy, sucky Blaise forever.

It would be easier just to quit. I don't even want to skate anymore. I get knots in my stomach just thinking about going back to the rink. Once I'm there I'm scared to move. I know that whatever I do, he'll start yelling at me. Of course, if I do quit, my mother will just harp on and on about my ungratefulness, my laziness, how I had one chance of doing anything worthwhile with my life and I threw it away, yadda-yadda-yadda. My future is bleak.

Mother and I are currently having a 'business lunch,' meaning that she talks about her plans for my future and I ignore her. Thankfully Blaise is absent, so I don't have to ignore their googly eyes or his creepy come-ons.

She's talking about interviews, and something about a more mature image. (What, does she want me to pose for Playboy or something?) I'm thinking about Doctor Bancroft, the specialist I saw in Toronto. He said that my competitive career was over. He said I'd be lucky if I even walked again. He's one of the best in the field; my mother wouldn't send me to second best. So how did he get it so wrong?

I'm thinking that maybe he didn't. Maybe he lied. I'd been seeing him on and off for about three years, not for anything as serious as a torn ACL, but athletes do get injured a lot. I always really liked him, and I think he liked me too. He told me once that he regretted being swayed by the siren call of money to choose a specialization. He would have liked to be a general practitioner, he said, the kind of doctors who goes on house calls and gives lollipop to well-behaving children.

Maybe he lied to protect me. Maybe he realized then what I'm starting to see now, that nothing short of a career ending injury would get my mother off my back. I know I was happier when I thought I wouldn't skate again than I am now.

Another injury is starting to look really tempting.

CHAPTER 15

Blaise informs me that we will be working on triple jumps today. I'm not exactly eager but, then again, I'm not eager about anything lately. What's the worst that could happen? I'll fall and hurt my knee again? So what?

Still, I feel obligated to speak. "For the record, I'd just like to point out that my doubles are still shaky. I don't think I'm ready to jump a triple yet."

"Well, for the record, I'd like to point out that if we wait until your lazy ass is ready to do anything I'll be taking my retirement before you ever compete again! You think those sissy doubles are going to get you a medal? Now jump!"

"Do what he says, Susanna," adds my mother, of course.

Four more days. Today, tomorrow, Saturday, Sunday, which doesn't count because it's my day off, and Monday. On Monday evening, I quit. I'll deal with the consequences later.

I circle around the rink. I gear up. I jump. I spin. I land.

NO!

I can tell immediately that I landed wrong. I crumble in a heap on the ice, crying out in pain.

God, please, no. Not again. Please. I didn't mean it.

My mother and Blaise rush to my side. The pain subsides, degree by slow degree.

Blaise asks: "Are you okay?"

"I... I think so."

"All right. Get back up. Do it again, but better this time."

"What? No, I'm not going again. I'm calling doctor Kirby."

"Oh come on! Don't be a wuss. You just said, you're fine."

"I said I think I'm fine. I didn't go to med school. You didn't go to med school, either, so you don't get a say here."

"Don't be petulant, Susanna."

"I'm being responsible, mother. I'm going to call my doctor, and I'll stay off the ice until he gives me the thumbs up. Period."

***

Doctor Kirby is less than pleased by my phone call. He clears his schedule for me, though, and runs the whole battery of tests on my leg.

"I don't think this is too serious, thankfully," he finally says. "A little bruising, but no tears. I recommend keeping it iced and elevated, and stay off it for the weekend. I'll take another look Sunday afternoon."

"All right."

"Susanna, I wish you would be more careful; you're the one who has to live with your body and with the consequences if you push too far."

"I know that. I do, really. It's just... Sometimes..."

"Look," he adds hesitantly, "I know it's not my place. I hope I'm not out of line when I say this. I think you're a brilliant athlete, and I would hate to see your career cut short due to... shall we say, mismanagement."

"I appreciate that." And I do, both the sentiment and the effort at tact. "I think the extra days off will do everyone some good, put things in perspective again."

I think no such thing. In fact, I'm pretty sure that things will only get worse after a few days off. But Doctor Kirby has nothing to say in return, and I just go home.

***

Back home for the next stretch of the play-offs. One win, one loss, so even if we win both games at home (make that when we win both games at home) I'll have to go back for the next game.

I expected Anna to be at the airport, part of the welcome wagon. But she isn't. Ava warned me this would probably happen, but I hadn't believed her. Alright, so Anna has been more distant lately; our phone conversations are always getting shorter, and she texts more than she calls. But still, I thought she would be here today.

"What the hell, sis?"

"I don't know. Ever since her mom came to town, she's been weird. She's freezing us out. I don't know what to do."

"Three to one says her mom's mind-fucking her," adds Chuck.

"Thank you, Captain Obvious. That doesn't tell us how to get her back!"

"She's not a stolen toy or a lost puppy, Ava. It's not about getting her back, it's about her coming back."

"But she's our friend, and she's hurting. We have to do something."

"Like what, kidnap her? She's smart enough to realize how toxic her mom is. When she does, we'll be there for her. That's all there is."

Ava doesn't agree, and the girls continue to argue all the way back to their place. Once we reach the building Ava storms out of the car, in a huff. I also get out, telling the others that I'll make my own way back to my place. I want to talk to Anna.

It takes her a long time to open the door. "Luke," she says when the door does open. "You're here." She sounds incredulous.

"Yeah, I just got back into town. Are you okay? You didn't come to the airport."

"Well, um, I guess it's complicated."

I don't like her tone, or the way she hedges around the question. I ease into the apartment, and I see it, on the couch: cushions piled on both ends, and an ice pack on a small towel.

"What happened?"

She's closing the door of the apartment, slowly. Almost like she's using the action as an excuse not to look at me. "Yesterday, in practice, I tried to jump a triple and I fell. Adrian said to stay off the ice, and to keep my knee iced and elevated for the weekend. He'll take another look again on Sunday afternoon."

She fell, yesterday. Hard enough to call a doctor, hard enough that she has to take a break in her program and stay off her knee for days, and she didn't tell me.

"Why didn't you call?"

She's facing me now, but she's staring at the floor, still not looking at me.

"I... well... I didn't want to bother you. You were out of town, there was nothing you could do about it anyway."

"I don't care that I couldn't do anything. If it was serious enough for you to call Doc Kirby-"

"He's my doctor."

"Yes! And I'm your boyfriend! If you get hurt bad enough to call a doctor, then I have a right to know. Otherwise, what are we even doing here?"

She's looking at me now, with her eyes bulging out and her face turning white.

"What?! No, no, please don't go, please." She's crying now. Damn it, I hate tears. I reach out my arm to her, and she grabs onto me, clinging for dear life. "Don't go, please. I'm sorry. I'm so sorry. Don't go."

"I'm not going anywhere. I just want you to talk to me. It's okay, honey, just stop crying." I don't know why I say this, when has that ever worked, but I can't think of anything else. Of course, she keeps crying. "Let's get you back on the couch," I eventually say, because I figure she's been on that leg long enough. I pick her up and carry her, setting her down as carefully as I can, putting the ice pack back on her knee and making sure she's comfortable.

Finally, as I kneel down next to her, the tears stop. She's still gulping in huge breaths, but it's already a lot better. "Anna, please. Just talk to me. What is going on here?"

A few more gulps of air, and she answers. "My life is such a mess. My mom is being horrible to me; she hired this new coach I hate, and I'm pretty sure it's just because they're sleeping together. Every time I do something that he doesn't like, which is all the time, she just backs him up. She's treating me like a broken skating robot. It's like November all over again."

"What do you mean, November?"

"Last November, she took me to the rink. I was still walking with crutches, there was no way I could skate. I figured she was just taking me there to 'keep my head in the game' or whatever. She took the crutches and told me to walk on the ice. I didn't want to, but she just kept pushing and pushing, making more and more ridiculous arguments, like 'it's just like walking on black ice', you know, and eventually she just pushed me on the ice. I fell and couldn't get back up, and they had to call an ambulance. My old Doctor told my mom, then, that I wouldn't be able to skate anymore. That's why I came to Winnipeg again, Adrian was the only doctor who agreed to see me."

I can't believe what I'm hearing. "Wait, back up a little. You're saying that your mom literally pushed you back on the ice? A month after you tore your ACL?"

She nods. This is ridiculous. This is fucked up. "Anna, you have to fire her."

She looks hesitant, which is just one more thing I can't believe. "But she's my mom."

"Who cares about that? We're talking about your well-being, here. About your career. As your manager, she's supposed to look after your career, and she's not doing that. It was pure dumb luck that you didn't wreck your knee completely last November, or even yesterday. A good manager would have done their best to stop those things from happening; she actually made them happen. You don't have a choice."

She just stares at me for the longest time. I think she's going to try to argue, but that's okay; I know I'm right, and I'm not backing down this time. But eventually, she nods. Good. I guess I got through.

"I know a lawyer, a specialist in sport contracts. I'm going to call him, see if he has some time to see us this weekend. All right?"

She nods again.

***

Luke is right. I don't like it, but he's right. I have to fire my mom.

I tell myself that, over and over again. While he's calling that lawyer he knows. While we're driving out to meet him. While we're sitting in the waiting room. While I'm shaking he lawyer's hand and answering his questions.

"No, I don't have a copy of the contract I have with my mother. It's probably stored at our bank in Toronto."

"That's not a problem. The contract must be registered in order to be valid. Once we finish signing the paperwork here I'll be your attorney on record, and I should be able to access it."

Luke is right. I have to fire my mom. Luke is right.

"No, I don't really know how the money works. I know that there are some grants, and that I've been getting sponsorships, especially since I started going to the World Championship and the Olympics, but I don't know where that money goes."

"I think it would be prudent, at this point, to hire a forensic accountant, to verify the state of the accounts."

"Do you really think it's necessary?"

"It would be better to have solid evidence, if we need to sue for mismanagement of funds."

"You mean like theft? You think she's stealing from me?"

177

"I'm suggesting that we should be prepared for any possible scenario."

My mom could be stealing from me. Of course she could. I feel like an idiot for not having seen it before.

I have to fire her. Luke is right. I have to fire my mom.

"All right, everything is signed here. I'll get to work on those court orders. Everything should be ready by Tuesday morning."

Luke asks: "do you think you can make that Monday morning?" But I speak up quickly, before the attorney can answer: "Actually, Tuesday would work just fine, thank you."

"Tuesday would work just fine?" Luke asks once we're back in the car. "Anna, you're not backing out are you?"

"Monday is the last day of the Blaise try-out. I'm going to tell her, tell them both, that I'm not going to work with him anymore and that I want my old coach to come here. If she doesn't listen to me, then I'll come back for the papers."

"And if she does listen to you? That Blaise guy wasn't around when she pushed you on the ice last November."

"Maybe he was. I have no idea how long they've been seeing each other. I want to give her one last chance. She's my mom, Luke."

"Do you really think she's going to listen to you?"

No. I don't. "I want to."

He sighs, exasperated, but he doesn't say anything more.

I know he's right. I have to fire my mom. But I really don't want to. Monday will be the test. Maybe she'll give me a reason to trust her. Maybe, just maybe, I won't have to cut her out of my life.

CHAPTER 16

The weekend goes pretty well. We win our two home games, as predicted. We'll have to leave for the fifth match on Wednesday, but that's further down the road. Cross the bridge when you get there, and all that.

Anna and I spend almost all our time together. She comes to both games, and sits with Ava and Chuck, but it doesn't look like they talk to each other much. I ask her why, on the way back from the third game.

"I don't know. I guess it's something my mom said, about how you guys are only hanging out with me because I'm famous. She said that when you realize how busy I am with the training and that I can't always hang out with you, you'll get bored and not want to be my friends."

That, right there, is exactly the kind of thing that pisses me off about Anna's mother. The way she's messing with her head, the way she clearly doesn't care about her. Even my dad was never that bad.

"And you actually believe her?"

"I didn't want to. It's just, she said that after she told me I wouldn't be able to go to the last game of the regulars. When I called Ava to tell her that, we sort of got into a fight. She came to apologize, but things have been awkward since."

This is bad. Anna's too insecure, too wrapped up in her mom's bullshit to try to fix things with Ava. But like Chuck said, it's not like we can kidnap her for a reverse brainwash. It has to come from Anna.

"Maybe you should talk to them, Ava and Chuck. You should tell them what your mom said." I'm suddenly getting a vivid mental picture of Chuck's reaction to Anna's story, and I snort.

"What?"

"Nothing. Just, when you do tell them, especially when you tell Chuck, make sure I'm there to see it."

"Now I'm really nervous."

"It's nothing bad, I promise."

I can tell she doesn't really believe me, even though I mean it. I'm sure Chuck won't actually, physically harm Anna. I let the subject drop anyway. We drive in silence for the next little while.

"Luke," Anna eventually says, "you mind telling me where we're going?"

"Just a bit out of town. Don't you think it's about time I showed you where I live?"

"You're taking me to your house?" Good. She sounds happy about that. Excited, even. "You don't live in town?"

"Nah, I live on the other side of the highway. It's only, like, half an hour away."

"That's still pretty far, considering how early you have to be at the rink, and for how long."

"It goes well enough. Roads are pretty empty at those hours. The worst is when we're flying in or out of town. When that happens, I usually crash with either Pierce or Dom. They live closer to the arena."

We have basically reached my house by that point so I stop at the beginning of the driveway, to give her the full view of the house.

"So, what do you think?"

"I don't know." My heart drops to my stomach. She hates it. "It's kind of short on windows, and balconies."

I can't really describe the sound that comes out of my mouth then; half laughter, half sigh of relief. My house is pretty much all windows and balconies.

"Well, you win some, you lose some. I do have a three-car garage."

"Really?! Where?"

"Right here." And I drive under the house, to the three-car garage.

I give Anna a tour of the house; the space in front of the enormous windows, which is an awesome room to take in the view but not really much else; the tiny kitchen and eating bar; the guest bedroom; and the Master, which takes up all of the second floor. Though, to be honest, that would be more impressive if the second floor was more than half as big as the first floor.

"It's funny, I didn't take you for a 'kooky-shaped house in the woods' kind of guy."

"Well, you know, I've been living in cities my whole life, sharing my space with a bunch of people. I wanted my own. And I figure, if you're going to have a house, might as well have one that makes a statement."

"This one does, that's for sure."

I feel like a wimp for asking, but I want to hear her say the words. "So, do you like it?"

She turns and faces me with a big, sunshine smile. "I love it."

Awesome!

***

Sunday afternoon, Doc Kirby comes by to examine Anna. He tells her that, if she feels up to it, she can go back to training on Monday. Of course she feels up to it, or so she says, and so I drive her to the arena Monday morning.

A woman is standing at the entrance of the arena. She has dark brown hair, like Anna had on the Friday we met, and she barely looks forty. A bit on the young side to be the mother of someone our age but, still, I have a hard time figuring out who else it could be.

"This is a private session," is the first thing she says. "You need to leave."

"Good morning, Ms. Miles. I'm Lucas Crawford."

"I know who you are. As I've already said, you need to leave."

"Mom, do you really have to take that tone? Luke isn't going to hurt my concentration; I've skated in front of him before."

"Get on the ice, Susanna. We've lost enough time as it is."

"Mom!"

"It's all right, Anna." It's not like I expected her mother to act differently with me, not with what I knew about her. "Call me when you're ready for me to pick you up?"

She nods. I lean down for a quick kiss, and am almost immediately yanked away by Ms. Miles. "I'll walk you out. Susanna, I don't like repeating myself. Get on the ice right now!"

It's not like either of us has much of a choice. Anna waves me goodbye as she walks backwards in the direction of the ice, and I return the wave as her mom drags me to the door.

Once we get to the parking lot, Ms. Miles turns to me. "How long to do plan on letting this go on?"

"What are you talking about?"

"This... flirtation you have with my daughter."

I have to admit, I didn't expect that question. "Are you... asking me if my intentions are honorable?"

"Do you think I was born yesterday? Of course your intentions aren't honorable. As if you would actually commit yourself to a long-term relationship with my daughter. She has no time to dedicate to romance, and you must have other, more... convenient opportunities that would suit your needs better. I'm asking when will you finally put an end to this farce, so that our lives can return to normal as soon as humanly possible?"

What... did she just call me a man-whore? She thinks she can just say shit like that and I'll disappear, so she can go back to bullying and hurting Anna freely? She has another thing coming.

"Normal? You mean like when you pushed Anna back on the ice one month after she wrecked her knee, risking permanent damage? That kind of normal?"

She doesn't even look ashamed when I say that. If possible, she only looks even snootier. "My relationship with Susanna isn't any of your-"

"Not my business? Oh yes it is. Anything that could hurt Anna is my business. Because, and that's the difference between you and me, I care about her. And I'm not going anywhere."

I turn and walk to my car, before I do something drastic, like punch her.

I drive around for a while, trying to calm down. I'm thinking about going to the gym and sweating out the anger when I get a text from Anna. She needs me to pick her up, now? She's only been gone 10 minutes, tops. Something happened.

***

I'm worried about what my mom is saying to Luke right now, but I try not to focus on that. It's the last day with Blaise, so I'll do what my mom always tells me to do. I'll focus on my skating, and I'll think about fixing whatever damage she did to my relationship with Luke at the end of the day.

Blaise is in full form this morning. I don't know if it's because I spent four days away from him, but he seems even worse than usual.

This time, I can't stay quiet.

"I am so glad that today is the last day we're working together. You are the worst coach I've ever met!"

"Well, I'm sorry if you have a problem with my attitude, princess. Maybe if you worked your lazy ass instead of just lounging around, we could make some progress."

"And maybe, if you somehow manage to make some of your pathetically few brain-cells connect, you would realize that just shouting insults at me isn't going to fix whatever imaginary problem there is with my skating. But what am I saying? It's not like you can give any constructive criticism; you clearly know nothing about skating!"

We stare at each other, in silence. I really don't like the look on his face right now. Maybe I pushed him too far.

"Come here," he finally says.

"Why?" I really, really don't like the look on his face.

"I said, come here!" When I don't make my way toward him fast enough, he skates up to me.

"You want constructive criticism? You want me to tell you exactly what's the problem with your skating, and how to fix it? The problem with your skating if that you are too stiff. You need to loosen up."

And then he grabs me, pulling me right against him with both hands on my ass. I immediately shove against him, as hard as I can. "Get off me!"

"Woo, girl, you've got some spunk. I like that. Spunky girls are the best lay."

"I said get off me right now!" I manage to get enough distance between the two of us for one good kick, and I use it. God bless the toe pick, it helps make the kick especially efficient. I get away and off the ice just as my mom returns.

"Susanna. What are you doing?"

The literal answer to the question is that I'm taking off my skates. "I'm going home. And I'm not skating with him anymore." I grab my bag, stuff the skates in it, grab my jeans and yank them on. "The experiment is over, it failed, and I expect you to call Liam and get him here as soon as possible."

"Experiment? We made a deal, Susanna, and you still owe us the three days you took off this week."

I've just slipped my boots on, so I stand and face my mother, whipping my jacket on, ready to get out of the arena at the first opportunity. "First of all, mother, those three days were a medical leave, which was brought about by the fact that you both insisted I make a jump I was not ready for. So I owe you nothing. Second of all, I refuse to work with someone who plays grab-ass with me."

I expect her to be shocked and angry when I say that, and she is, but there is something else. She looks hurt. Well, of course she's hurt. A man she trusted and cared about made a pass at her daughter. I guess that's a good show of how low our relationship has sunk, that I didn't actually expect her to care about that.

She turns toward him. He's managed to skate to the edge of the rink, next to where we are.

"Blaise? Is that true?"

"Of course it's not, baby. She came on to me. Of course I turned her down right away, and I guess she didn't like the answer, and now she's trying to ruin my reputation."

What bullshit! Does he really think it's going to do anything except make him look even worse?

Only, my mom turns to look at me again, and that look is more painful than anything else she's ever said or done to me. The hurt is all gone, replaced by anger. She doesn't care about me. She cares about him. She's taking his side over mine.

"You're not serious," I say, a little in shock. "You're going to believe that? Believe him, over me. I'm your daughter!"

"And I'm your mother, and your manager. That you would behave in this manner with your coach, a man whom you know I care greatly about? It hurts me, Susanna, on a professional level as well as on a personal one. I expect better from you."

"All right, you know what? Whatever! I don't have to listen to this. My point stands: I'm not skating with him anymore. I'm going home. I'll come back tomorrow morning, and if he's still here I'm turning right back out and leaving."

I text Luke on my way out. He looks really mad when he comes to pick me up but I'm still too shaken up by what just happened to ask about it, or to talk about anything else.

"Wanna talk about it?" He asks, and I shake my head.

"I can't yet. Can we walk? Can we find a place to just... walk? I need to move, I need..."

I'm gesticulating, trying to find the words, but Luke gets what I mean even if the words don't come. He drives to a park, and we walk up to a bench. He sits down, and I try to do the same, but I can't stay still. I just keep getting back up and pacing in front of him.

"Anna," he finally asks, "what happened?"

I try to tell him, but the words don't come. After about a minute of opening and closing my mouth, like a fish, I finally shake my head. "Can't. Can't yet. You first."

"Huh?"

"You're mad about something, or you were when you picked me up. What did my mom say to you?"

I probably shouldn't have brought this up, because he looks angry again. He shrugs. "She asked me when I was planning to break up with you, so your life could get back to supposed normal. I'm not, by the way."

"I believe you. So that was it?"

"Mostly, yeah. There was also the bit about how I couldn't be serious about you because I'm such a man-whore. I mean, for real? She says stuff like that?"

"Well, back when she was telling me that Ava and Chuck aren't really my friends, she said that you couldn't be serious about me because I don't put out. It's all the same thing, sort of."

"Still, what kind of mother says that, to her daughter's boyfriend?"

"The kind of mother who sides with her lover when he molests her daughter."

Luke stares at me, slack-jawed, while I keep pacing. "What?"

Now that I've started, it's easier to go on. Not by much, but enough for me to go on. I tell Luke everything that happened at the rink this morning, everything that was said and done.

"Anna!" He says when I'm finished. "This is serious! You should have called the cops. You need to call them right now."

"No. I can't."

"What do you mean you can't? You just said he molested you. He belongs in jail."

"I don't have any proof, Luke. It'll be a bunch of he said, she said. If my mother decides to back him up, and it looks like she will... And if it gets out, the publicity would be terrible. Besides, he's gonna be gone tomorrow."

"You can't know that!"

"I'm pretty sure. Why would she take the chance of leaving her slutty daughter alone with her boyfriend?" Struck by the irony of the situation, I can't help but snort.

"Isn't it funny? I'm too prudish for my boyfriend, but too slutty for hers." Except that, when I say it out loud, it doesn't sound funny anymore.

***

The next morning, Luke drives me to the arena once more. He argued about me spending the night at his place, or him spending the night at mine, because he didn't want to leave me alone. It just didn't seem practical, so we came to a compromise: we told the girls, and they flipped a coin to figure out who would spend the night on my couch. Chuck won.

The three of them spent most of yesterday trying to convince me to go to the police. It didn't work. I can't risk the publicity. I just want him to go away, and I'm sure that he's already gone.

I wonder if there is a point in my life when my mother will stop surprising me in unpleasant ways. He is still there, standing next to her, when Luke and I walk inside the arena.

"I thought I made myself clear, mother."

"We had a deal Susanna. And from now on, I expect-"

"I don't care about what you expect. The line has been crossed. I told you what would happen if he was still here this morning."

I leave the arena, Luke right behind me. "What now?"

"Now we go to the lawyer. Enough is enough."

He probably figures that 'enough' had been reached a long time ago, and that this is more along the lines of 'better late than never,' but he doesn't say anything.

When we return to the arena, Mom is standing alone and looking very displeased. That sight, earlier this morning, might have been enough to make me relent and convince me that our relationship was salvageable. Now it's just much too little, much too late.

"Blaise has gone back to the hotel. I hope you find the success of your bout of childishness satisfying. I, for one, must admit that I think your lack of professionalism is very disappointing."

I say nothing in return, merely walk up to her and give her the legal papers I had been holding.

"What's this?"

"The legal dissolution of our professional relationship. From this moment, you are no longer my manager."

She looks stunned. "You're not serious?"

"The accounts are frozen, while a forensic accountant is looking over them. I hope that there is nothing to be found. I wish I could be sure there isn't."

"I do not appreciate this prank, Susanna. Even if you ever had the gumption to do such a thing, it would be impossible to do in less than 24 hours."

"The papers were signed last Friday."

She might not have believed what I was saying before, but she sure does now.

"This is absurd! You can't do this to me. I'm your mother!"

"And apparently, that means as much to me as it does to you."

"I sacrificed my skating career giving birth to you."

"You were an eighteen-year-old novice who never got on a podium, six weeks away from your nineteenth birthday, when you learned you were pregnant with me. You had no career left to sacrifice. And don't think that I don't know that if there had been any chance of you ever having a real career, you would've had an abortion."

"I should've had one anyway, considering the lack of gratitude I'm getting from you. I gave you every opportunity, the best this business had to offer. You don't have a career without me."

"Maybe I don't! Maybe I'll have to do something else with my life. Maybe I'll become a Starbucks barista, or a Walmart sales associate. Maybe I'll make the reality television circuit, like Dancing with the Stars, or Hollywood Squares. Maybe I'll write a book, an exposé about my life and my career under the wings of my manager/mother. The kind of book I could write about you would make Joan Crawford eligible for a Mother of the Year award. And who would want to work with you then? Because the truth is, maybe I don't have a career without you, but you sure as hell don't have one without me."

She freezes over at the accusation, with an expression not unlike that of her boyfriend yesterday. "We'll see about that," she says, and she storms out of the arena.

Well, I did it. I fired my mother. And I have no idea what comes next.

CHAPTER 17

Luke spends all of Tuesday with me, except for the one hour he spends going to his house, grabbing his overnight bag, and coming back to my place.

"I have to spend the night in town anyway, because we're taking the plane super early tomorrow."

I know the real reason he's insisting on spending the night here, rather than with Dom or Pierce. He's afraid that my mom's boyfriend will hang around in town and decide to try something. I tell him that he doesn't need to worry; with both him and mom fired, they have no reason to stay in town. Besides, he's never even been to my apartment. But Luke insists and, in the end, I agree because his presence is comforting.

He leaves the next morning, promising to win this one and be back soon. Ava is driving him and the other guys to the airport, so she stops by my door to tell him it's time to go.

"Anna, why don't you come on up? We can have some breakfast when I get back, have a talk."

She grabs Luke and leaves before I can think of a good excuse to say no. I haven't been alone with the girls since the night my mom dropped by my apartment. I'm sure things are going to get super awkward.

I suppose I could just stay downstairs until Ava gets back. Maybe I'll think of something before then. But that would just be putting off the inevitable. Ava is Luke's sister, she and Chuck spend a lot of time with him. As long as Luke and I are a couple, they will be a part of my life. Ava and Chuck have reason enough to be mad at me, it's only fair to give them a chance to let it out.

Maybe things will be less awkward afterward.

If something is going to be done it might as well be done soon and, in this case, soon means now. So I climb up the stairs and knock on their door.

Chuck opens it right away. "Hey! Come on in. I'm making pancakes, there's enough for three."

I come in, I sit down, I watch as Chuck continues to make breakfast, I stay silent. Eventually, she turns to me. "Are you just going to sit there and not say anything, because this could get awkward."

"Well... I figured I should wait for Ava. I'd rather not repeat myself."

I'm not sure that Chuck understands me, but she doesn't let that phase her. After a short pause, she answers "okay," and goes back to making pancakes.

Ava does return, after what feels like an eternity. She and Chuck set the table, chatting about the guys and the upcoming game, like this morning is nothing out of the ordinary. Once everyone is seated and served, Ava turns to me. "So, what's going on with you?"

"I fired my mom yesterday."

"Hallelujah."

"Chuck!" Ava's admonition doesn't seem to upset Chuck, who shrugs while Ava puts a hand on my shoulder. "Are you all right, sweetie?"

"Yeah. I mean, it had to be done."

"It's about what happened the day before yesterday, right?" I nod, and Chuck continues. "I figured as much. I still think you should call the cops."

"Luke too. I told you before, I don't want the publicity."

"You don't want to make waves, and that's on you. But sometimes, you have to make waves to stand up for yourself. I mean, look at us. Your mom told you to stop spending time with us, and you listened because you didn't want to fight with her, and nobody was happy."

"That wasn't it. She said you guys didn't really want to be my friends, that I was a conversation piece to you, because I won a silver medal at the Olympics, and that when I started getting serious about my training and didn't have as much time to spend with you, you wouldn't want to hang out anymore."

"Excuse me?"

"It was the night before the last regular season game, right, when you and I had that fight? Oh, that is just sucky timing all around. Anna, it's not true. We date professional hockey players, we understand the demands of sports. And it's not your Olympic medal we find interesting, it's you."

"I know that."

"No, I don't think you do," Chuck says, and I suddenly remember that Luke wanted to be there when I told the girls about what my mom had said. I have a feeling I'm about to learn why. "So let me make it very clear. You won a silver medal at the Vancouver Winter Olympics. A lot of people won silver medals in those same Olympics, including the US men's hockey team, who lost the final game in overtime. Do you know who scored the goal that sent the game into overtime? My boyfriend, Pierce Bristow. If I wanted to brag about anyone's Olympic Silver medal I would brag about his, not yours. I'm hanging with you because I like you. Got it?"

I nod, feeling really embarrassed that I listened to my mom on this. I didn't know about Pierce's medal (but I bet Luke did, and we're going to have a discussion about that in the near future) but I still should have known better. I should have trusted my friends.

"Good. Now, when are you calling your old coach?"

"I don't know."

Ava responds by asking: "how much time do you have? I don't suppose you can go into competitions without a coach, but I guess you have until summer, right?"

"I don't know if I'm going to call him. I don't think I want to compete anymore." That is an understatement. The idea of even going back to the rink is making me nauseous. I realize that it's my mom's boyfriend and his crap coaching that are messing with my head, but the point remains. I don't even want to skate right now, let alone compete.

"But," Ava sputters a little before she can speak again, "but you have to compete. If you don't, your mom wins. It's like you fired her for nothing."

"I didn't fire her to start a competition between us, I fired her because I couldn't work with her anymore. If she wins anything by me not skating, it's a victory by forfeit."

"But-"

"Shut up, Ava. If Anna doesn't want to compete anymore, that's her call. It's not like we only hang with her because she's a skater, right?"

"No! Of course not. But Anna, skating makes you happy."

"Not lately, it hasn't."

"All right. So you have issues to work through. Work through them. It's your life to live, and you can't be expected to make any kind of major decision over a plate of my awesome pancakes, even if they are a gift from the gods."

We all laugh and really start eating. I don't know if I would go as far as calling them a gift from the gods, but they are some really good pancakes.

***

For the last two days, I haven't been doing much of anything. I've mostly just been sitting on my couch and moping. I'm getting really tired of myself, and my body is starting to protest against the lack of activity. This has gone on long enough. I need to move on.

What do I do now? That's the question I've been asking myself since January. I feel that I'm back where I was at that point: with my career behind me, and no plan for the future.

I look at the bedroom wall and I see something that's been there all along, but that I haven't looked at in a long time. The plan I made to get back in control of my career, and of my life. So much on that list depends on my mom no longer micro-managing me. She was the biggest obstacle all along; why did it take me so long to see? And, now that she's gone, why am I still letting her influence me so much?

I remember the reasons I had to start training again. If I can't, that's one thing. But I know I can. And if I don't, I'll always wonder what might have happened. I'll always hear my mom in my head, calling me a quitter. Telling me that I don't have a career without her.

Well, we'll see about that!

I run to the phone and I call Liam.

"I'm surprised to hear from you," is the first thing he says to me.

"I know it's been a long time. I'm sorry."

"How's that new coach working out?"

"He's not. He's out. And so is my mom. I fired her."

"Did you, now?"

"Yeah. It's a long story, and I guess it's not really that important. The thing is that, right now, I sort of don't have a team, and I kind of need you. You said you would come here, the last time we talked, right?"

"Right, but that was before Olivia fired me three weeks ago."

What? She did what!? "She... fired you? Three weeks ago?" Before she came here with that boyfriend of hers. She'd already fired Liam, and she flat out lied to me about it.

"I've been looking for a new skater."

Of course. That's why she insisted on a two weeks trial for the other guy. She wanted to make sure that I would have no choice but to work with him, because Liam would have found another skater by that point.

"Did you find one? Please tell me you didn't. I don't want to have to find someone new. I need someone I can trust right now. I know I'm being childish and unfair, but please tell me you didn't find another skater. Please tell me that you still want to be my coach."

"I haven't found anyone else. Season is only just wrapping up, no one is in the market yet. As for coaching you... I don't have any problems with you, Susanna, you know that. But I've been in the business long enough, I've paid my dues, and I've earned the right not to work with people like Olivia Miles anymore. Now, if you're telling me that she's out-"

"She is. She's out, she's gone, she's never coming back, I promise. Does that mean you're coming?"

"I'll fly over this weekend. We start on Monday. Send me the address of your rink, I'll meet you there at seven AM."

I'm so grateful that I'm practically in tears by the time I hang up. The conversation I just had with Liam just circles around in my head, and I start pacing in my apartment without even realizing it. Once I do realize, I stop myself, only to start and stop again. Clearly I can't stand still. I need a walk. And, in fact, I know exactly where to go.

Twenty minutes later, I have made my way to Chuck's garage, and I'm in her office.

"My mom fired my coach, three weeks ago, and she lied to me about it. I asked her point blank, and she lied to me."

"Of course she did." She says that like it was obvious, as if I had said 'The sky is blue' instead of 'My mom lied to me about firing my coach'. "What would you have done if she'd told you the truth?"

"I would have quit."

"And I bet you told her that. So she said what she needed to say to make sure you didn't quit. She's an abuser, Anna. It's the typical pattern, she's always putting you down, cutting you off from other people and making you dependent on her. The important thing is that she's out of your life. That's a good thing."

"I know, but damn it, Chuck. It's not supposed to be that way. She's my mom. Why doesn't she love me? Why can't she care for me the way she's supposed to?"

"I don't know, Anna. I don't have any experience with that kind of relationship. You've met my parents, you know how they are. I can share them, if it makes you feel better." That makes me smile. "Luke and Ava might be able to understand better. You know about their family, right?"

"Not really. I'd figured out that there's something, but they've never told me, and I didn't ask."

"Well I guess it's their business, to tell you when they're ready. How'd you learn about your mom firing your old coach, anyway?"

"He told me, just now."

"You called him?"

Chuck has a funny smile on her face right now. "Yeah, I called him. What?"

"Nothing. It's a good step. I'm proud of you. So are you coming tomorrow?"

"Where?"

"To our place. I guess Ava hasn't called you yet. We're planning a little something, to celebrate the boy's victory. I'll let her know you'll come. Our place, 7:30."

***

I want to go to Ava and Chuck's party with Luke, but it just turned 7:30 and I don't see his car. I text him and he says to just go on ahead, he'll catch up with me.

The truth is I catch up with him, and with everyone else. They are all waiting in the apartment when I show up, ready to yell "Surprise!" and to sing the birthday song.

"How did you all even get here without me seeing you?"

"I never reveal my secrets, grasshopper." Ava puts a party hat on my head and, once it's secured with the elastic, she blows a party blower in my face.

"You know you actually missed my birthday, don't you?"

"Yes, I know, I'm a few days late. But your mom was here on your birthday, and that's not conducive for a party mood. Besides, better late than never."

I make my way to the couch, through the noise makers and the party blowers. I sit next to Luke, and look at the party fare gathered on the coffee table. There is a cake, a card, and a wrapped present. I notice a theme.

"Alice in Wonderland?"

"Yes," answers Ava. "Because you, my dear, are Alice. A young girl, who finds herself in an enchanted place, meets extraordinary companions, finds herself facing the evil Queen of Hearts in a deadly game of chess, and emerges victorious."

There was no way this group was going to let that metaphor go by unscathed.

"Wait! Are we the extraordinary companions? Who's who, then?" "I call dibs on the Mad Hatter, he's cool." "You're more like Tweedledee and Tweedledum." "But wait! Alice didn't have companions. She meets people on the way, but she's always traveling alone." "What's that about the Queen of Hearts playing chess? I thought she played croquet." "No, wait, there is a queen who plays chess; I saw it in one of the movies. I don't think it's the Queen of Hearts, though." "There are two evil queens?"

It's too much for Ava to bear. "Can't you people just accept a metaphor without ripping it to shreds? The point is, Anna, you need to read your card, open your gift, eat some cake, and then call your old coach."

"Is it okay if I do it out of order? I already called my old coach, yesterday. That's what your smile was about," I add, pointing to Chuck, who takes a very dignified pose and answers, "I have no idea what you are talking about."

Pierce breaks the tension. "Why don't we just forget about all that and eat cake?"

That sounds like the best idea right now. We eat the cake, and it's delicious. I read the card, everyone wrote a nice little word, even Adrian and Grace. I open the present: it's a pair of skates, but not traditional skates, I'd never be able to wear them in competition. They are all black, they reach higher than normal skates - a good five inches over my ankle - and they have little decorative buttons down the sides. They are supposed to look like Edwardian style boots, to keep with the Alice in Wonderland theme, and I love them.

I can't remember the last time I really celebrated my birthday. It's a tradition I'll be glad to pick up again.

CHAPTER 18

I spent the whole weekend at the rink, running drills by myself. I needed the time. I needed to push Blaise's voice out of my head, so I could be clear and ready when Liam arrives on Monday. I have no idea how good, or bad, I look, but I feel better than I've felt since my mother showed up on my doorstep.

When Liam arrives on Monday, I'm as ready for him as I could be. I run drills, much like I did with Blaise. But, unlike Blaise, he doesn't criticize my every move. He doesn't even comment; he just calls out one move after the next. After about two hours of this, he calls me back to the bench where he's been sitting.

"So?" I ask him. "What do you think?"

"I think your jumps are shaky, your endurance is shot, and you look like you've forgotten how to hold your positions. You're not competition ready yet. That being said, you're in better shape than I thought you'd be. So we have five months to get you back to top shape. Up for the challenge?"

"Yes, sir, I am."

We spend the rest of the day working. By the time he calls it off, at around six, I'm really tired. It's a good kind of tired, though, like I've done something valuable today. Things are falling in place now, and I know that I can do this. Once I'm home, I look up the competitions for the next year. I take notes, trying to figure out which ones I should register for. It's the sort of thing that my mother always took care of, but I'm sure I can figure it out. I'll ask Liam to help me tomorrow.

I also need to figure out my routines. One thing I know for sure is that Julia Nader's stuff is not for me. I didn't get the chance to use the numbers I'd planned for this competitive season, so they are still a possibility for the upcoming season. The short program will probably have to change a little, to allow for this year's required elements.

Or I could create something completely new. I've always liked choreography and, even before this whole mess began, I was toying with the idea of making my own. Now would be the best opportunity to play with that.

So things are pretty good, professionally. But, personally, I'm not doing so well. I can't forget the look on my mom's face when she walked away. I have to fight myself not to call her, to try and make peace with her, basically every day.

I don't know what happened to us. Was our relationship always this bad? Was she always more abusive employer than affectionate mother? I remember she was always pushy, but it seems to me that things weren't so bad before Vancouver. I could be wrong about that, though.

Sometimes I try to remember the life we had with my dad, when we all lived here, before the divorce. Somehow, it looks so idyllic; skating on frozen ponds, playing in the snow, drinking hot chocolate afterward. Too good to be true, right? And maybe it was. Maybe I made it up.

I'm thinking about my dad, today especially, because Lucas is telling me about the next steps of the Stanley Cup championship. Right now, the Jets are in the semi-final of the division. If they win, they go on to the division finals.

From the way things look with the other semi-final pair of the division, the odds are good that the Washington Capitals are going to advance to the division finals. That team name actually rang a bell, but I couldn't tell exactly how or why, until the boys started teasing Luke about a guy on the Capitals he apparently really doesn't like.

"Admit it, Luke," says Pierce. "The reason you want to go to the finals is to beat Owen Stark out of a chance to win the Cup."

Owen Stark? I know that name. How do I know that name?

"It doesn't hurt, I'll admit."

"Wouldn't it be a shame if after all this, the Capitals don't even make it to the finals."

"If that happens, it just means that I beat him by being a part of the better team."

"Oh!" I remember where I've heard the name before. "I know him! Well, not really know, know," I add when I realize that everyone is staring at me. "My dad mentioned him, once. He's the son of one of his best friends."

Which brought to mind the conversation I had with dad last month. And it's all I can think about.

I say this to Luke, when we're back at my place. "I don't understand. He calls me, out of the blue. We talk about a bunch of stuff, you and Owen and stuff. He brings up my mom, then, after we hang up, he calls mom to complain about the fact that I complained about her? It doesn't even make sense!"

"The logical answer would be that he didn't call to complain about you."

"But why would he call her at all? She would have no way of knowing that I talked to him if he hadn't called her, and she couldn't have guessed the subject of our conversation unless he told her. Why would he do that?"

"Maybe he was trying to defend you, to tell your mother to ease off or something?"

"But why now? I've hardly heard a peep from him since my tenth birthday. Why would he choose now to start getting involved in my life?"

Before either of us can guess an answer to that question, the phone rings.

CHAPTER 19

I'm sitting in the lawyer's waiting room. This is a little annoying, actually. He called me, saying he needed to talk to me, I show up at exactly the right time, and I still end up waiting. It's always the same thing. At least Luke is there to keep me company.

"So, what's the story with you and Owen Stark?"

"Oh, that. Well, it's nothing, really. Well, not nothing, it's just... we made it look like a bigger deal than it is. We're the same age, Owen and me, recruited the same year, and we never really liked each other. It's like he's always after me, saying just the right thing to piss me off. It wasn't so bad, at first. He signed with Washington right away, and he stayed with them. At first, I'd signed with Nashville, so we weren't even in the same conference. We shared the ice maybe twice a year, more or less. But then I signed with the Jets, and we're in the same conference, now.

The same division, even, so the teams play each other all the time. Let's just say all this time together didn't make us any closer."

"Ah."

I'm not sure what to say to all that, and the lawyer arrives and lets us into his office before I get a chance to figure it out.

∗∗∗

"Now, Miss Miles," says the lawyer, "I have the report from our forensic accountant back. Let's start with the good news; your accounts are in good order, and have been for several years."

"So my mother didn't steal from me?" Well, that was a relief. She's not completely selfish, heartless, and evil.

"What do you mean, for several years?" asks Luke.

"Well, there were some suspicious withdrawals, about twelve years ago."

Twelve years ago. I would have been eleven. "But none since?" That doesn't make sense. My parents had already been divorced for two years, I was alone with my mom. If she had stolen from me once, successfully, why didn't she just keep at it? "Is it possible that there was a misunderstanding, twelve years ago?"

"It's possible, although, to be completely honest, I rather doubt it. More likely, it was your father's intervention that put an end to the theft."

"My father?!"

"Yes. I have here the court transcript from that period. Your father went back to the court, and demanded a more stringent supervision of your mother's expenses, and of your accounts. The supervision would cease once you reached eighteen years of age and took back control of your money. Your mother, it appears, agreed on the condition that your father abandoned all visitations rights."

My father did that? For me?

That's why he called her the other day. He wanted to know why she hadn't turned the accounts over to me, the way she was supposed to.

"But why didn't the accounts go back to Anna's name when she turned eighteen?"

"This is where things get a little tricky. Your mother claimed that there was a verbal agreement between the two of you, that you preferred she remained in charge of your account. I assume that no such agreement existed?"

I shake my head. "We never talked about it, so I guess that means no. But then, what stopped her from robbing me blind for five years?"

"The accountant in charge of supervising your funds refused to turn over the account unless you came to the office and signed the transfer paper in front of him. So your mother kept paying herself a salary of 50% of your gains, rather than risk losing everything. It was a lucky break, really. But the claims of a verbal agreement make the legal case against your mother problematic, should you choose to pursue this."

"I don't want to sue her. She's locked out of the accounts, now, right? Everything is in my name, and she can't touch the money anymore? That's all I want."

Well, that and to talk to my dad again.

***

I'm sitting in my living room, holding my phone in one hand and my dad's new number written on a piece of paper in the other. I've been psyching myself out about calling him for half an hour. I need to do this. Yeah, he might be at work, or out with friends, or busy. I still have to call him. I can always leave a message, but at least I'll have taken the step.

Quickly, before I can change my mind once again, I dial the number. It rings, three times, before the line clicks open.

"Suzie?"

"Hi, dad."

"Hey. How's it going?"

"Pretty good." I think about making some more small talk, but decide against it. I only have so much courage. "Listen, dad, mom came over, last month."

"She went to Winnipeg again? What, did hell freeze over?"

"Maybe. Maybe it was that phone call you gave her that motivated her. Why didn't tell me that you gave up visitations rights to make sure mom couldn't steal from me anymore?"

There is a long silence at the other end of the line. "She told you all that?"

"No, the lawyer I hired to fire her told me, after he had a forensic accountant look into the money thing."

"You fired your mother?"

"Yeah, it's a long story. There was that new coach she'd found, and a lot of other things. Anyway, it's done."

"Suzie, I'm so sorry. I hoped things wouldn't get that bad."

"But you thought they might? Then why did you leave me with her? You could have taken me away; I'm pretty sure that you could have made the case that a mother who steals from her child shouldn't have sole custody."

"I was trying to do the right thing by you, Suzie. I didn't want you to have to quit skating."

"What are you talking about?"

"When I learned about what your mom was doing, I'd already moved back here. There aren't any fancy skating clubs, or coaches, or choreographers, or anything like that. All that stuff's in Toronto, where you were with your mom. You have to understand, baby, I've never seen you happier, or more proud of yourself, than when you were on the ice. Even when you fell, it only made you more determined to get back up and do it right. It's your calling. I know about callings; you don't become a cop without one. My calling is the law, yours is skating."

I have to think about this for a minute, to try and find the right thing to say. "Dad, I get what you're trying to say, but I have to wonder if you made the right decision. I won't be competing forever. What am I going to do for the rest of my life? Maybe if I'd gone with you, I would be better prepared for a normal life."

"You mean, going to high school, and then to college, and then getting some job somewhere? You'd have been better prepared for that, sure, but where does it say that that life is better than the life you're living? I've watched every competition of yours that ever played on TV. I've got them all recorded. And I tell you, Suzie, you still have that same look on your face when you skate. I see you so happy, and so proud, and I can't think that I've made a mistake. As for the rest of your life, you can do anything you want."

"Come on, dad. That's cheesy."

"No, I mean it! There's that guy, the one who went to the Olympics, Elvis something, I heard he's on Broadway now. You could get on Broadway. You can do anything. And whatever you decide to do, I'm proud of you."

That's even cheesier, but it feels so good to hear.

After hanging up, I look at the pile of documents I picked up from the lawyer. All the money things. My mind cannot even process the size of the numbers on those papers. I'm going to need an accountant, for sure, but I'd like to be able to follow along with those papers. I don't want to risk getting robbed. Again.

I wish I'd paid more attention to the math tutor.

CHAPTER 20

I can't imagine what Liam wants to talk about when he calls me over that day after the training is over. I have a feeling that I won't like the subject. The session went well though, so what could he have to talk about?

"We have to start thinking about your future."

"Okay," I say hesitantly. "What about my future?"

"People have been calling. Journalists. Your mother was spotted back in Toronto and, with you still here, rumors have started circulating that you're retiring. You'll have to start thinking about an official statement."

"Right." I wonder if my mother herself couldn't have started those rumors. Proving in her own twisted way that I really don't have a career without her.

"Saying that you're back for the next season won't be enough. You'll have to register for the upcoming competitions, plan your calendar, settle on your routines. You'll need someone to deal with your sponsors, and with all your expenses. You need a manager."

The words fill me with dread. "I thought maybe we could figure it out. I mean, if I get an accountant for the money and I keep working with the lawyer Lucas introduced me to, I thought maybe with them and the two of us..."

"Look, Anna, neither of us has a head for business. There's no shame in that. Of course I'll help in any way I can. And the accountant and the lawyer are good ideas; the more people you have working on smaller pieces, the easier to keep everyone in check. But you need someone who's good with business. Someone you can trust."

"I trusted my mother, look where that got me."

"Fair enough. You should have been able to trust your mother. But that's done now, you have to move on."

He senses how uncomfortable the idea makes me, and he pushes. "What is it?"

"My mother, before she left, she said I didn't have a career without her. I know, I know," I say when I see his face. "I don't really believe it, either, not intellectually. But, in my gut..."

"All right, just listen to me. You're not going to be able to do this on your own. That doesn't mean you need your mother, specifically. That means you need someone. I'm going to give you some names, all right? People I trust. Take a little time, think about it, then call them."

"Okay, I will."

"And think about your routines some. We're going to have to change the short program anyway."

"Do you think I could try to make some new numbers, by myself? We used to talk about that."

"I remember. Give it a try, see what you come up with."

***

We lost. In four games. While Washington is well placed to move on to the next round. I bet Owen Stark is looking at the sports section and laughing his ass off at me, and that really burns.

Oh well. On to the next season. At least I've got a nice vacation to look forward to.

"I'm so sorry," Anna says. That's another thing that helps to swallow the pill, a girlfriend full of sympathy.

"It's fine, I promise. Losing happens. We'll try again next season."

She looks at me, a little suspicious. "Are you really as Zen about this as you say you are?"

She's a really funny one. "Yeah, mostly. There's just... well... If the Capitals go forward, and they probably will, Owen Stark will be unbearable next season. I'll have to kick his ass a few times to teach him a lesson. It's all good."

The suspicion melts into amazement. "I don't know how you do it."

"How I do what? Not freak out over not winning the Stanley Cup this year? I'll have other years, and I've got other things going for me."

"I guess that's something I need to work on."

She looks really sad at this. We need a distraction. I tip my glass and drop some of my drink on my shirt. "Oh, shit!" I hope I wasn't too obvious.

"Oh, God! Are you okay?" Apparently I wasn't. Good.

"Yeah, I'm fine. I just need to get this off." And off the shirt goes. Is it a cheap trick? Yes, but I'm doing it to myself, so it's not as bad. Besides, judging by the way her eyes glaze over, I'd say it's a success. She's not sad anymore.

"Hey! What's that?" She grabs my arm, tries to twist it and look at my inner bicep.

"We saw each other in bathing suits, you know," I tease. "You didn't notice my ink then?"

"I was distracted by Pierce's massive work of art. Come on, let me get a better look."

I hold my arm out. She traces her fingers over the black and white *fleur-de-lys*, and the words written underneath.

"*Je me souviens*," she whispers under her breath. "I remember. Remember what?"

"That's the question, isn't it? It's the motto of the province of Quebec. No one knows exactly what you're supposed to remember, which is some irony. You just, well, remember."

"That's sweet." She looks up to me. "You look so sad."

I guess I do. I feel pretty sad. "I just miss home, sometimes." I wish she would do something to distract me. My awesome girlfriend is basically sitting on my lap, and I'm trying to figure out what I did to make my father stop loving me. It's pathetic.

She takes over the distraction business pretty well, though. She presses her lips against mine, and soon there's nothing but her.

***

I eventually man up, so to speak. I call the names on Liam's list, leave messages. We'll see how it goes. He's right, I can't do everything by myself; I need someone I can trust. But learning to trust a complete stranger... Well, Liam trusts them, so I guess I'll just have to get over it.

In the meantime I try to focus on the one thing I can do myself, choreography. My mother never wanted me to. "Focus on your skating, Susanna." Well, screw her. I am focusing on my skating, just a different aspect of my skating. I will do this, and it will be awesome, and that will show her.

Except, right now, I've got nothing. I don't know if it's because I want it too much, if I'm jinxing myself or something, but it's just not coming.

I try to go back to the basics. I listen to all the music in my collection, searching for inspiration.

But all the songs I hear are either unusable, meaning that they are over four minutes long or that they have words (what are those doing in my library anyway), or I've already skated to them, or I don't like them (and what are THOSE doing in my library? I need to clean up, seriously).

There are a few exceptions; some Celtic numbers that I really like. I remember my dad playing these around the house when I was little. My mother always hated them, which is a double motivation to use them. The problem is, I don't think Liam likes them either. He's always been very cautious when I bring the subject up, saying that those are high endurance numbers, and that endurance isn't my strength.

I agree with him, up to a point. But for the short program, I think I could handle it. I really do. And I don't want both programs to be too similar anyway. Only all the Celtic numbers I have are four minutes long, if not longer.

So I've got nothing, and I'm not feeling good about myself right now. I need a distraction. My first reaction is to go to Lucas, but I don't want to be one of the girls who lives for their boyfriend. And that's when Ava calls me. I tell her my problem and, while she finds my exasperation amusing, she suggests that we compare our music collections.

"I have this enormous collection, for work. You never know what a bride might choose for her wedding music, so it's better to be prepared for everything. You might have something I've never heard, that I could use, and vice versa."

I was hoping to be done with music for tonight, but spending an evening with Ava and Chuck is always a good time. I don't really expect Ava to have the perfect pieces of music for me, but I'm happy to help her if I can.

So we're listening to all sorts of music, debating their merits. Our collections are a lot more similar than the girls expected; it gets really amusing when I begin to list all the songs I've skated to in the past. And then, the most beautiful piece of music begins to play.

"Hey, what's that?" I ask.

Chuck flips the CD to look for the answer, but Ava is faster than her: "It's Pachelbel's canon in D."

It's amazing. How have I never heard this before? I love it! "How long is it?"

"It depends on the version. This one is about nine minutes. Most versions are about that length, too."

Shoot! That's way too long.

"Are there any versions shorter than that? Like, around four minutes?"

"I've never heard any. But that would be way too short for a wedding. It takes more than four minutes for the bridesmaids to walk down the aisle. I'm probably going to have to play this one in a loop as it is, and-"

"Ava, get on with the program. Anna found a song to skate to. Didn't you?"

"Not if I can't find a four minute version."

"Well, how hard can that be? It's a canon, the whole point of canons is that they are an infinite loop. If you cut a few loops, it'll sound just as good."

I hope she's right. I really want the song to sound just the way it does right now. I can see myself skating to it. I have the movement, and I even have a basic idea of the costume. I grab a pad of paper and a pen, and I begin to make notes before I forget them. Meanwhile Chuck is on the Internet, looking around for a four minute version of the canon.

"Well, I guess that the wedding planning section of the evening is over," Ava sighs, before she grabs her own computer to help look around. "You know," she adds, "if we find a four minute version that you can't get on a CD for some reason, I know a lot of musicians, and at least one guy with a recording studio."

"Really? You would do that for me? Do you know anyone who could help with costumes, too?"

"Please! I've got so many designers in my Rolodex, I have no idea what to do with them all. You can have as many of them as you want."

"You're an awesome person to know, Ava Crawford."

"Which you already knew, Susanna Miles. Or at least you better have already known."

When Chuck finally finds a four minute version of the canon, on Youtube, of course, Ava's generosity seems especially inspired. I'm really lucky to have those two girls as my friends. And when I tell the girls about my desire to use a Celtic number for my short program, they come up with the idea to use only a portion of a number. They even help me find the perfect number.

And it really is perfect. Once again, as soon as I hear it I know it's the one. The choreography almost designs itself. I discuss choreography and costumes with the girls, and they are both so excited it's contagious. I'm finding the joy of skating again, thanks to my friends, and I'm so grateful for them.

I spend the rest of the night planning. Liam is going to be shocked when he sees me tomorrow. I'm so ready for him.

CHAPTER 21

When I present my programs to Liam the next morning, he's not exactly impressed at first. And, to be fair, the plans I have on paper aren't what you would call impressive.

But they work, I know that they do. I just have to convince him.

"That canon song," he eventually says, "how long does it last?"

"I found this version that lasts three minutes and fifty four seconds. I don't have a proper CD of it, but this friend of mine works with musicians, and she knows someone who has a studio, and she says she could get me in touch with them and help me get a CD. She also knows designers, who could help me with the costumes."

"What kind of work does this friend do, anyway?"

"She owns a wedding planning business."

"Oh."

"Anyway, I've got great ideas for the costumes-"

"Hold on, honey, let's back up a little. What about that other song, Cry of the Celts? It says here that it's over four minutes long."

"I'd just be using the last two minutes or so."

"And it's one of the Riverdance numbers you like so much, isn't it? The ones your mother never let you skate to? Now look, Anna, I know it's tempting right now to rebel against your mother, and do everything she ever told you not to do, but in this case-"

"It's not that! I mean, okay, it is a little, but it's not just that. My dad used to play this music around the house all the time. I love these kinds of songs. And I can see the choreography in my head, Liam. I know it can work."

"It would be a high energy number, Anna. You're not a high energy skater."

"I can do it for two minutes! Just let me show you. Let's try it right now." I know he'll never understand unless he can see it.

After what feels like forever, he nods. I plug the song into the speakers of the arena and wait for my cue. I know, even as I'm skating it, that the routine doesn't look like what I had envisioned. But it feels good. I feel good, strong. I can tell I've got something special here. I'm so immersed in the dance, I'm not even thinking about it. It just comes so naturally. I'm preparing for the double Paulson, and I know I've got just the perfect prep. I make the decision a fraction of a second before I jump. I rotate, once, twice, three times, and I land perfectly. It doesn't even hurt, or feel sore. It feels wonderful! The last few seconds of my routine probably look like the ugly end of a dog, but I don't care. I'm still on a high. I've jumped a triple!

"Liam! I jumped a triple."

"So I saw. Think you can do it again?"

"Yeah!"

"Good. Because we have a lot of work to do to get this number competition-ready in a little less than five months. Show me the other one, the canon."

And I do. I'm still feeling high from the triple. I can't wait to call everyone and tell them. My first successful triple since my injury. It feels glorious.

***

A little later that week, I meet Grace for lunch. We haven't had a chance to talk, really, since before my mother came into town. I'm glad she invited me, although I'm also a little cautious.

"So," she asks me after the general niceties have been exchanged, "How is the skating going?"

"The skating is going well. The business side of things is more problematic. I don't know if you know, my mother used to be my manager, and, well, I had to fire her."

"I'm sorry to hear that. It must be difficult. I can only imagine the impact on your relationship."

"We don't really have a relationship anymore. For a while, really. I try not to think about it too much. There are more immediate concerns. The business end of things is getting overwhelming, really fast. I don't know how much longer I can manage by myself before things begin to slip, and everything goes out of control. Having the lawyer and the accountant helps, but they have to refer every decision they make to me. I called a few potential managers that Liam, my coach, recommended. So far, everyone is busy or they don't want to move here."

"Perhaps I could help."

"You know someone?"

"I know myself."

"You?!"

"Don't sound so surprised. I used to work as a paralegal, so I know something about contracts and such. With the lawyer and the accountant, and some help from your coach, I'm sure I could manage. I already live here, and I was just thinking the other day that I was getting bored of doing nothing with my days."

It would be wonderful, but still I hesitate. She senses this and asks, "What is it?"

"Well, it's just... I do like you, very much, and I don't want things to change between us. Managing a professional athlete's career is a lot of work, I'm beginning to realize that. In those kinds of situations, little annoyances can grow into huge problems. It killed my relationship with my mother. The point is, it might be easier working with a stranger. I don't want to risk another relationship."

"I suppose that's up to you. The offer is still open, if you ever change your mind."

That's all we say on the subject, and the conversation awkwardly veers off in another direction. But my mind is still on our talk, and on her offer.

I can't believe what I just said. I can't believe what I'm doing. I would really like to work with Grace. It would probably be more sensible to choose someone who's been in the business longer, who has more experience and contacts. But I feel comfortable with Grace. I think working with her would be fun. And I'm letting my mother scare me away from that? No way!

The next morning, I call her back, invite her to come to the rink and meet Liam. They hit it off right away and, less than twenty four hours after the original offer was made, I have a new manager.

CHAPTER 22

I spend the next month or so settling into a routine. I train a lot, I work on my new numbers, and I spend what time I can with Luke, Ava, Chuck, Dom and Pierce. They asked about coming to practice and watching me skate, and I said, "Fine, but let me know beforehand". I've had an idea, not too long ago, about a new exhibition piece, and I want to keep it a surprise to the gang. I even made Grace promise that she wouldn't mention it to Chuck.

Anyway, it's not at all unexpected when Ava comes to my practice, the first Friday of July. She does surprise me, however, when she asks if I can take tomorrow off. "I have plans I'd like to include you in," she explains. It's all very mysterious, but it doesn't sound bad. I turn to Liam, who is sitting next to Ava and has heard everything.

"Is it okay? I can come on Sunday to compensate."

"Oh, just take the weekend. You've earned it, and with the season starting up, you won't get many more chances to take a vacation."

Ava is thrilled, and instructs me to be ready at 9:30 and to wear "something that's appropriate day-wear." So, on Saturday morning, I put on my nicest summer dress and cutest sandals and hope that it's good enough. The girls are dressed in much the same way I am and the guys are wearing long-sleeved shirts and khakis, so I guess I look all right. We all pile into Pierce's SUV and Ava gives the directions to a country club just outside of town, which apparently serves the best brunch in the prairies.

Pierce takes the driver's seat, and starts to complain almost from the moment we leave the driveway. "We're not actually driving 45 minutes for a brunch, are we? It's too early for brunch. And it'll still be too early for brunch when we get there."

"It's not just a brunch, no. There's something we have to do first."

"Why didn't you just schedule the other thing after brunch? We could have slept one hour more."

"I couldn't; the country club is hosting another wedding in the afternoon."

Pierce grumbles a little but does not comment further. Everyone else's ears perk up, though.

"What do you mean, another wedding?" asks Luke.

Ava doesn't answer, but both she and Dom are looking very smug at the moment.

"You're eloping?" Chucks sounds incredulous, and I don't blame her. If I could speak, I would probably sound the same. "What kind of wedding planner elopes?"

"The kind who doesn't want any of her contacts to feel slighted when she doesn't go to them for her own wedding. The kind with parents of the groom in Hungary who can't easily travel. The kind who wants to challenge herself and plan a wedding as quickly as possible. This whole wedding only took 30 minutes to arrange. And by the way, some congratulations would be nice!"

With such an obvious prompt, of course we congratulate them both. Ava seems satisfied.

"Oh, also. I need you guys to decide now who will be the witnesses. We can only have two on the wedding contract."

"As the brother of the bride, I would like to withdraw myself from contention, in order to avoid overwhelming the wedding party."

"Dude, it sounds better if you just say 'Not It'."

"Shut up, Pierce."

"Hum, I think I should count myself out, too. It's more fair if Chuck and Pierce get to witness; they've known you guys longer."

"All right. Chuck, Pierce, you have a problem with that?"

Chuck and Pierce do not have a problem with that. We reach the country club at the expected time, and we meet Timothy Taggart, the minister Ava found to perform the ceremony. It's very simple, very nice. In front of us all, Ava and Dominik promise to each other that they will stand by the other's side, for as long as they live.

That's what marriage is, at the core of it. It's not about crazy gestures, or color-coordinating flower ribbons to bridesmaid dresses, or all this other stuff that Ava talks about when she tries to explain her job. That's the wedding. A marriage is about being with someone else.

I look over at Luke. I can see myself having that with him. I can't see much into my own life, past February, but I see him there. I see us going on dates, and I see myself cheering for him at his games, and him cheering for me at my competitions. I might not see forever with him, I don't even see forever with myself, but I see the foreseeable future. I'm ready to show him, and to take the next step with him.

After the brunch, which is very nice indeed, Ava and Dom announce that they have a room at a nearby hotel and that they'll see the lot of us on Monday. Chuck shrugs, grabs Pierce's keys, and offers Luke and I a ride back to town.

"Actually," I say, turning to Luke, "we're not that far from your place, right? Do you mind if we get a cab and head up there?"

He doesn't mind, and so we go.

Once we get there, I grab him and kiss him. He doesn't seem to mind, even if he looks a little bit quizzical when we stop to breathe.

"What was that about?"

"I love you. I've never told you before, have I?"

"Not in so many words." He smiles and leans down to me, looking me in the eye. "I love you," he says, just before he starts kissing me again. He'd never said it, in so many words. In fact, I can't remember the last time I heard the words. I forgot how good they felt.

When we next break for air, I look him square in the eye, and I tell him. "Luke, I'd like you to take me upstairs."

It takes him a minute to process what I'm saying. "Oh. Oh! OK. Are you sure?"

"Yes, I'm sure."

He studies my face for a little while. Something in my expression must convince him that I mean it, because he grabs him in his arms and carries me up the stairs.

***

I can't understand what my life is, right now. This morning, Ava eloped. Ava, my little sister, who's started cutting pictures in wedding magazines when she was six, who made it her business to plan weddings, literally. She eloped, just like that. She wasn't even wearing a white dress!

And now, twelve hours later, I'm lying on my bed next to Anna, and we're both naked. And she has a tattoo!

I'm rubbing the tip of my finger on the purple flower on her hipbone.

"You getting over that yet?" I don't even need to look up to know that she's smirking; I can hear it in her voice. Go ahead, babe, laugh it up.

"How did it happen?"

"Well, you go to a place that's called a tattoo parlor, and in those places there are guys - also girls, but generally guys - who have these machines with needles and ink and they-"

I pinch her, right next to the flower, not hard enough to hurt, but just enough to get her to stop jerking me around. "You know what I mean," I say over her squeals and laughter. "You're not the kind to just get a tattoo. There's a bigger story here. Spill."

She calms down, catches her breath. I guess the story isn't a funny one.

"Well, it was about four and a half years ago. I had qualified for my first World Championship as a Senior. I didn't win, I finished in either fourth or fifth place, I think. Anyway, I got some good press out of it, journalists were complimenting my grace and elegance. My mother said something about how it would be nice to get that grace and elegance embedded into my skin. I thought, 'that sounds like a good idea, actually.' I looked up different symbols of grace and elegance, but I didn't like any of the ones I found. Then I looked up flower language, and I came up with this; the jasmine, grace and elegance. I went to the tattoo parlor first chance I got. I chose the hipbone because I wanted to be sure I wouldn't have to take special measures to cover it up in costume, or in a bathing suit."

She's teasing me, but I can't bring my head into the game enough to return it.

Wow, her mom has been messing with her for a long time. Right now I wish I had a time machine, so I could go back in time and yank little Anna away from that messed up situation. Still, I know I can't say that; it'll just make her sad.

So I say the first thing that pops to my mind. "I thought that jasmines were white." That was so stupid.

"Mostly they are," she says, and her smile is still a little sad. "But they also come in other colors. I got purple because it's the color of royalty, pride and success, and I wanted those embedded into my skin as well."

"More like, you wanted to take what was inside and bring it outside."

She gives me the brightest smile when I say that, and then she grabs my face and starts kissing me again. Okay, then.

The important part is that she's not sad anymore. She shouldn't be sad today. It's been a good day. Weird, but good.

CHAPTER 23

I'm in a pretty good mood when I get to the rink the next Monday. That good mood lasts right up until the moment I see Liam and Grace, sitting together, looking sternly at me. Grace is holding a rolled up magazine in her hands.

"What is it? What did I do?"

"You didn't do anything, Anna, sweetheart. It's just, well, Liam and I learned a piece of news this morning. We figured we should break it to you, before you hear it from someone else."

"And I'm telling her that it's useless because you probably had a phone call from the press this weekend and you know everything already. Ain't that right?"

"No. Well, maybe. I haven't been to my apartment this weekend, I've stayed with Luke. I just went through for five minutes this morning, to grab my stuff. I didn't check my messages."

Liam and Grace are raising their eyebrows at me, in a 'oh, you spent all weekend at your boyfriend's place, did you, well we know what you did there' way. It makes me want to squirm a little, but instead I stand firm, with my chin up. Yeah, I spent the weekend having sex with my boyfriend, and I had a really good time, too.

"Well," Liam eventually says, "you've probably got a bunch of messages. Don't answer them, Grace is handling it."

"We can work out some statement if it makes you feel better, honey. But otherwise, 'no comment' should work well enough."

"Well enough for what? What's going on, here? Why would journalists be calling me, why would I need a statement?" Then it hits me. "Did my mom do something?"

They don't answer. Grace just hands me the magazine. It's the latest issue of *International Figure Skating Magazine*. Staring up at me from the glossy cover is Cicely Novak, the fake blond with the fake tan my mother pointed out to me last Nationals. According to the headlines, she is the next big thing in figure skating. Which is all fascinating - no, not really - but I don't see what it has to do with me, and I say that. Grace only opens the magazine to the right page, and points to one paragraph.

The paragraph details the changes Cicely made in her team for this season. In May, she hired the power-team of Blaise and Olivia Darrow as her coach and manager, respectively. Mrs. Darrow is the former Olivia Miles, mother and ex-manager to three time world champion, Olympic silver medalist Susanna Miles. She married Blaise Darrow in April.

"She married him? She married him in April?!"

"That's the part that upsets you?"

"Well, yeah!" I stare at Liam, who looks incredibly dubious. What, is it really such a surprise that I'm upset because my mother hardly even waited a week to marry a man who molested me?

Then I remember. Liam doesn't know that. Neither does Grace, who looks a little incredulous.

"Well, the day before I fired my mom, the new coach she'd brought with her, that guy," I add, pointing to the article as if they hadn't already figured it out, "he... came on to me." It's a mild term for what he did, but I don't want to have the whole "you should call the cops" conversation again. "I turned him down, and when I told mom, he said it happened the other way around. She believed him, which is bad enough. But then she married him, almost right away. Like there was no doubt in her mind. It's just... insane."

"Oh, sweetheart." Grace rubs a hand on my arm, and doesn't say anything else. What else is there to say?

"What about that skater? You realize she didn't get on the cover of IFS by accident. Your mother is probably leading a pretty savage publicity campaign. Right now she's focusing on bringing her skater up, but if she decides to turn nasty on you-"

"She won't. She'd think it's unprofessional. She's going to treat me like I'm beneath her notice. Well, she got the skater she wanted at least."

Grace asks: "What do you mean?" I repeat my mother's comments from the last Nationals.

"She could be right," Liam points out.

"Maybe, but I'm not freaking out about that. Our styles are too different. I can't become Cicely Novak, and I wouldn't if I could. I'll just focus on my thing, and hope it'll be good enough. Can we move on to the practice now?"

I'm really anxious to be skating, all of a sudden. I have something to prove. My mother is throwing down the gloves, and I have to pick them up. At some point this season I'm going to be competing against Cicely Novak, and I have to win. That's the only way I'll be able to prove to my mother I have a career without her.

CHAPTER 24

I am more determined than ever to have the best performance I can have. I spend almost all my time at the rink and, when I'm not there, I'm training at the gym, or I'm perfecting my routines, or I'm meeting with the designers Ava introduced me to and working with them on my costume, or I'm working with Grace and Liam to keep up with the business side of things, or I'm talking to the press. My life revolves around the competitive season.

The next thing I know, it's September. The summer is gone, and I didn't even see it happen. Luke and the guys are busy with the pre-season camp for the NHL, and the only reason I know that is because Ava comes to my apartment to tell me how much she misses her husband. She doesn't even live two floors up anymore - she moved in with Dom during the summer - she drives across town to come to my place and complain.

Not that I never spend time with Luke, but it's almost always when we are going out with the others. When it's just the two of us it seems like too much of an effort to go to his place, and when he comes to mine he often finds me surrounded by paperwork or asleep on the couch, or both. I don't like where this is heading. My season is important to me, but so is my relationship with Luke. I need to make a better effort at balancing them.

In the spirit of that effort, I drive up to his place to have a talk.

"Hey, stranger." He greets me with a smile, his voice a bad imitation of a Southern accent. "Long time since I've seen you around these parts."

"Have you been watching a western?"

"Well, a guy's got to do something to keep busy when his little woman won't visit."

"I know, I'm sorry."

"Kidding, babe." He drops the accent as he opens the door wider. "Come on in."

We walk up to his couch and he sinks in with a heavy sigh, eyes closed.

"Long day?"

"Yeah. I should keep in better shape during the summer, then September wouldn't hit me as hard. And how's your life?"

"Still busy. Wait until I start to travel; that'll be fun. So anyway, I was thinking we should spend more time together."

He opens one eye and stares at me with it. "Yeah?"

"Yeah. We're a couple, and we've hardly spent any time together since Ava's wedding. Our schedules are only going to get worse. We're going to have to make an effort, a commitment to spend more time together. Like, we could agree on an official date night once a month."

"That's an idea. Or you could move in here."

He closed his eye again, and now he's just lounging on the couch, very nonchalantly. Doesn't he realize what he just said? "I could move in?"

"Yeah. I'd make you a key and, when I'm not feeling so incredibly beat, I could call up the guys and we could pack your stuff and move it up here. Then, instead of dragging my ass to your place, or you dragging your ass to mine, we would both just be going to our place. We wouldn't have to go out on dates, we could just stay in, watch mindless TV, get Chinese or pizza."

He's serious. He wants me to move in with him. In this great house I love. So it's a slightly longer drive in the morning. I can totally live with that. "Okay. Let's do it. Make me a key, I'll start packing, and when everyone has some free time, I'll move in with you."

"Awesome." He's still got his eyes closed, and with the huge smile on his face, he looks fairly adorable.

"Want to practice for our future stay-at-home dates? I've got an overnight bag."

"Ooh, yes."

***

October, the beginning of the 2013-2014 season. I had been looking forward to that season. For one thing the new division line-ups actually makes sense, and we don't have to fly - or worse, bus - all over the place anymore. Even better than that, Washington is now a part of the Atlantic division, in the Eastern conference, and we're part of the Central division, in the Western conference. Which meant I wouldn't have the aggravation of playing against Owen Stark, unless it was to beat the Cup out of his hands.

But then, guess what the asshole did? He transferred to Chicago, in the Central division, in the Western conference, that's what. And now I have a pre-season game to play against him.

He starts on me as soon as we find ourselves face to face on the ice. "So you got a new girlfriend. She's cute. I should go introduce myself to her: with our dads being friends and all."

Does he really think he can get to me with that bullshit? That's pathetic. He used to be able to trash-talk better. Either that, or I'm becoming more mature.

Wow, that's a scary thought.

"She's not Talia, dude. She wouldn't go for your type."

"I could always make her."

All of a sudden, I see red. It's not Stark I'm seeing anymore, it's that creep Blaise Darrow. Putting his hands on Anna's ass, calling her feisty when she's trying to fight him off.

I spend a lot more time in the penalty than usual. Might have been worth it, only it didn't make me feel better.

***

The guys lose their pre-season game. On home ice, to boot, which is especially disappointing for Dom and Pierce. They argue that they would have had a better chance of winning the game if Luke hadn't started so many fights with that Owen Stark guy. Him again.

Luke doesn't say much to those accusations. He doesn't say much about anything. We're at Goodman's, taking some consolatory beer, and he's only staring at his glass, not even touching it. I need a break from the tension, and I excuse myself to the ladies' room for a few minutes.

When I come back out, there is a guy blocking the door. Six-foot-five if you include the extravagantly coiffed reddish hair, surprisingly small and squinting eyes that I think are blue, a look that probably aims for "smoldering" but lands in "smug". I am not impressed.

"Excuse me." I try to get past him, and he shifts his weight to block me. "Suzie Miles?"

Either he's incredibly cocky, giving me a nickname when we meet for the first time, or he talked to my father. It's the second possibility that allows me to recognize him. I am still unimpressed.

"It's Susanna."

"I'm Owen Stark."

"I know. You're in my way."

"Your father talks a lot about you. He's very proud. I can see why."

"I said, you are in my way. Move, please. I'd like to go back to my friends."

"Back to Luke Crawford? I don't think you should do that. You were at the game this afternoon, right? He's got some anger management issues. I'm saying that for your own good, I don't want you getting hurt."

"My relationship with Luke is none of your business, and now I insist that you leave me alone."

"Don't take that tone, Suzie. I'm just looking out for you. I feel like an honorary big brother of yours."

I respond with a strong: "you're not my brother, of any kind!" I'm not even sure he heard me, though, because Luke speaks up at the same time. Where did he come from? "She told you to leave her alone."

"I'm just making conversation, dude." But Owen's tone betrays his casual words. He's spoiling for a fight. "You got a problem with that? You gonna do something about it?" And he shoves Luke. Luke probably would have jumped on him if Pierce hadn't been right there to hold him off. Dom steps in front of Owen. This could get really bad. I have to do something.

"Luke, I want to go home."

That does the trick. Luke calms down enough for Pierce to let go of him, and he grabs my hand to drag me out of the bar.

**

"What is the story here? And don't give me the brush-off again. You and Owen Stark have a past, and it's affecting you now."

I can tell that Luke doesn't like the subject of this conversation, but also that he agrees with what I'm saying.

"What happened tonight was more about our present than about our past."

"Tell me anyway."

A big sigh, and he goes on. "My ex-girlfriend, Talia, she left me for Owen not long after I signed the contract with Winnipeg. Stark and I didn't like each other before, but that only made it worse."

"Oh, no. No wonder Ava hates her."

"Yeah. Anyway, he sort of implied, tonight, that you would do the same. Don't make that face at me. I know you wouldn't, and I said so to him. He said he could make you."

"He's a prick. But if you're really sure that I'm not going to dump you for him, why did you spend so much time tonight fighting him?"

"It's the making-you part that pissed me off. It was too much like that guy, Blaise Darrow."

"Oh." I don't know what to say to that. It's actually really sweet; he was trying to protect me. Should I be saying that I don't want him to fight for me, that I can take care of myself? I did take care of my mom's then-boyfriend-now-husband by myself, but I would have liked to have Luke there.

If he had fought the creepy coach my mom married, I wouldn't have stopped him.

"You know," I eventually say, "I bet Talia broke up with him, if it makes you feel better."

He doesn't look sure. "Where'd you get that idea?"

"He wouldn't have come so hard against you, using me, if he didn't have something to prove."

He thinks about that for a minute, and then he smiles. "You know what? It does make me feel better."

"You're my hero, Luke. Try not to let that jerk get the better of you, okay?"

"All right."

CHAPTER 25

It's time. October 18th, 2013. The first day of Skate America. My first competition of the season. I flew to Detroit, where the competition is held, with Liam and Grace earlier this week. The boys are playing an away game in Vancouver, and Adrian, Ava and Chuck couldn't take the time off to come with me.

I wish I could say that the loneliness that comes from missing my friends and my boyfriend is the worst feeling in my body. It's not. I think I'm getting a cold. My throat is raw and aching, and I'm feeling a little dizzy. Liam hasn't said anything, so I'm keeping quiet. If it was bad enough to affect my performance, Liam would have said so. I drink a lot of orange juice, I take some Aspirin and some Halls I grabbed at a pharmacy, I sleep as much as I can, and I hope for the best.

There's a small part of me that thinks maybe I should cancel this competition, go back home, and get myself back into shape. But I know I can't. I've already missed the entire last season, and with my mother waiting in the wings to make the worst of every situation, I know that if I don't skate this weekend my career is as good as over. I can't let that happen, I just can't.

I'm going to be okay. I can do this. I have to do this. I'm an athlete, a professional. I have endurance. I can power through. I'll be fine.

Through the practice, and the first day of competition, I repeat this mantra to myself. The short skate is a nightmare. I finish at the bottom of my group. It could have been worse, of course. I could have face-planted on the ice. I feel terrible.

I go back to my hotel room, completely dejected, trying to figure out if the biggest mistake was coming to this competition or not quitting skating last October.

I'm well into my pity-party, missing the girls and the alcohol they brought last time I had one of those, and most of all missing Luke, when my hotel room phone rings. "Miss Miles, this is Tiffany at the front desk. I'm sorry to disturb you, but there are two gentlemen asking to meet with you in the lobby. One of them is Mr. Lucas Crawford."

"I'm on my way!" I don't even care who the second guy is. Luke is here. I was just wishing for him and he's here. It seems like only a second before I'm throwing myself into Luke's arms.

"What are you doing here? I thought you had a game."

"I ditched. Like I was going to let you go back to your first competition by yourself. You were great out there."

"Luke, come on, I was terrible. If you saw the competition, then you saw the score."

"Those judges have no idea what they're talking about. You were great. And I know someone who agrees with me."

He stands a little to the side, and reveals the second guy the girl from the front desk talked about. He would be easy to overlook, especially standing next to Luke. He's much shorter, five foot six at the most, and not anywhere near as well-built, with fading, graying strawberry-blond hair. But I can't stop staring. It's the first time I've seen that face in fifteen years.

"Dad?"

"Hi, Suzie."

I have no idea what I'm supposed to do now. Should I hug him? Should I shake his hand, or something? Eventually, I suggest grabbing some dinner at the hotel restaurant.

"You were great today, Suzie."

I smile at Dad over my plate of spaghetti. "I was terrible, but thanks."

"I liked the song you picked. It's from Lord of the Dance, right? I love that show."

"Yeah, I remember. You used to play it around the house all the time. I've been wanting to skate to a number like that for years, but mom wouldn't let me."

"No wonder; she never liked me playing them around the house either. She doesn't like being reminded of her origins."

"Mom's Irish?!" How did I never know that?

"Her parents are. Or were. I didn't have much of a reason to stay in touch with them after the divorce; I suppose they could be dead. She never had a good relationship with them. I always figured that's why she never went back to her maiden name after the divorce. She didn't want to be associated with the Kennedy family."

I feel really sad at the idea that I have grandparents who might have lived and died without me having any idea that they existed. Mom never talked about her family. I wonder if she blamed them, the way she blamed me, for supposedly ruining her career.

"Anyway, I like your choice of song. You cut it short, though, didn't you?"

"Yeah. I really wanted to use that song, see, but there is a time limit on our routines. I thought it cut pretty well at the spot I'd chosen."

"It did. I think it takes an obsessive fan like me to notice that it wasn't the full song. What about tomorrow, what song will you skate to then?"

We talk about my program, and then about his job. Luke says very little during the dinner, unless directly addressed by my dad. I don't need his words, his presence alone makes me feel better.

The next day, October 19th, I skate the long program. It goes better than the short program, much better in fact. I finish fourth overall, and I am pretty satisfied with that result. I won't be skating in the exhibition program of this competition so I might as well go home a day early, which is what I do. I drive to my apartment, I call Luke to let him know that I am home, but that I'll spend the night at my place rather than his, and that I'll see him tomorrow. Then I go to bed.

On Sunday, October 20th, I don't get up.

It's not that I don't want to. I wake up, more than once, to the sound of my alarm, or of the phone ringing, or the doorbell. Every time I try to get up, and every time I fail, and fall back asleep again.

On one of the many wake-ups, I find Adrian examining me. He informs me that I don't have a cold anymore; I have pneumonia. I'm stuck in my apartment for the week. On most of the other wake-ups, I find Grace, or Ava, or Luke, sitting next to me on the bed. Once, I wake up cuddled to a plush white rabbit which is wearing a tag which says "I belong to Anna "Alice" Miles."

CHAPTER 26

It takes me a week to get over the pneumonia, and then I have three weeks to get back in shape. My next Grand Prix is the Eric Bompard trophy, in Paris, from November 15th to 17th.

I am not looking forward to this competition, for one very serious reason: Cicely Novak is also registered. Mom will be there, and so will her husband. I frankly don't want to see any of them.

I catch sight of them all at the arena. The husband is keeping his distance, so that's good. My mother looks right through me, like I'm invisible, which is pretty much what I expected. Cicely, on the other hand, has obviously noticed me. From what I can tell by her behavior, she wants to be sure I notice her as well.

"Susanna Miles." She smirks at me. I never liked her looks, now I can say that I don't like her attitude either. "Look at you. How'd Skate America go?"

"How are you, Cicely?"

"I'm amused. I really wonder what the point you're trying to make is. You were good, once upon a time, but really now. Every good thing must have its end. It's time to leave some room for the younger and better generation."

My mother harshly calls out to her. Cicely rolls her eyes and walks away. So no love lost there. Which is well enough, I suppose.

I skate better than I did in Skate America. Much better, as a matter of fact. I might have even ended up in first place, if not for Cicely. Turns out that Mom completely recycled her plan for me, including the Julia Nebar routines. Unfortunately, Julia's style fits Cicely like a second skin. Her scores are almost perfect, and she and I get gold and silver respectively.

Which means that I failed. At this first match-up between myself and my mother, my mother won. And she is very happy to let me know how she feels about that. Not through gloating, she leaves that to Cicely. Mom simply arches her eyebrow at me and walks away, leaving a hole in my stomach.

Liam and Grace do their best to cheer me up, but at this point there is only one thing that could make me feel better. I go back home, and gather everyone to finish the move the following weekend. Ava takes the opportunity to throw a house-warming party. The guys have prepared a set of Alice-in-Wonderland-themed good luck charms to bring with me to the Grand Prix Finale, in Japan, the first week of December. The party is a little over-the-top and ridiculous, and it's exactly what I need. All of my hurt at seeing my mother, all of my tension about the upcoming competition, where I am sure to see her and Cicely again, it all melts away.

When the first weekend of December comes, I am ready. Mom behaves much in the way she did in Paris, looking right through me. Cicely is a little different, though. Edgier, in a really strange way.

"Back for more, Susanna? You must love silver," she mocks when we happen to share an elevator at the hotel. "The Olympics, and last time, and now today. You just can't get enough of silver, can you? I prefer gold, and I'm going to get gold, because I'm younger, sexier, better than you!" And she laughs off the elevator.

What was that about?

If it was supposed to make me feel worse, well, it didn't work. I remember something my mother always said, that rubbing your victory in the face of your competition is a sign of insecurity and vulnerability. I'm guessing she didn't give that lecture to Cicely, or that Cicely didn't listen. In any case, I am now more confident than ever of my chances at winning.

I take the ice feeling more confident than I have in over a year, if not longer than that. My scores are similar to the scores at the Eric Bompard, only a slight improvement. The big difference this time is with Cicely. She takes that new edginess of hers on the ice, and makes a lot of little mistakes, losing just enough points to take her down to second place.

Our score is even now. Next stop, the Nationals.

CHAPTER 27

The holiday season comes and goes and, before we know it, it is January 2014. The Nationals are upon us. This competition will decide not only who goes to the Four Continents, or to the World Championships; it will determine the Olympic team.

The competition is in Ottawa this year, and will begin on the 9th. I flew in on the 8th, with Liam and Grace, and those of the gang who can come arrive early the morning of the 10th. They insisted on giving me some physical support.

On the 9th skaters have some practice time, and I find myself once again cornered by Cicely. This time she's beginning to turn nasty.

"You think that one victory means anything? You're done, everyone says so. They all think that you're pathetic. You're not going to the Olympics this year. It's my turn now. I've got the best manager, the best coach, and the best choreographer. I can get anything I want. All the titles, and all the guys. Even yours."

"Cicely, you need to stop. You're making an idiot of yourself."

"What, you think I can't do it, is that it? I took your mom's husband easily enough. That's right," she says, when she notices the face I'm making at the news. "I can get any man I want. I can do anything I want, and no one can stop me."

After that, she skates away. Boy, was that conversation weird. I'm not worried about what she said, that she would seduce Luke. I trust him. I do worry a little about the fact that she can brag about seducing her coach, her manager's husband, with no shame. She's welcome to the creep, but why would she want him? Yeah, she's eighteen now, so it's not technically illegal, but it's still all kinds of wrong. And beyond all that, there is something seriously wrong with that girl. I'm sorely tempted to keep an eye on her, and on everyone she talks to. She might try to pull a Tonya Harding on me.

***

It's Friday, three o'clock. The Women and Ice Dance short programs are scheduled to begin soon. Women skate in groupings of five and I happen to be in the first grouping, with Cicely, of course. Two of the other three skaters I know a bit from sight, Nicole Green and Christine Meilleur. The last skater of the group introduces herself as Audrey Lennon. It's her first time competing at the Senior level at the Nationals, she was immediately promoted after winning gold at the Junior level last year. She is 15 years old.

"I just wanted to say," she whispers to me when we get a few seconds standing next to each other, "I've been watching you skate for years, and you're my biggest inspiration. I want to be you, when I grow up."

"Wait, you mean you think that I'm grown up?" We both laugh at the joke, and it's good to be speaking to a fellow skater who doesn't actually wish me bodily harm. The other skaters are keeping their distance for the most part. I understand. I've always been pretty cold toward everyone I ever skated against, you can guess who's to blame for that. Besides, this is a competition, and we are here to win, not to make friends. Still, meeting Audrey is the best thing to happen to me at the Nationals yet.

I don't know if I'm carrying the high of having met her with me to the ice, but I skate my short program like I've never skated it before. It goes on like a dream, no, even better: it goes on the way I imagined it when I first wrote the routine all those months ago. When I finish, I know I have a perfect score. At the end of the day, the results are me first, Cicely second, Nicole third, Audrey fourth, Christine fifth.

The second day of competition is also a good day all around. Audrey is the first of the group to free skate, and she does so well that she actually takes the first place. In the past, that would have caused a spike of anxiety, "can I get the first place back", and so on. But not this time. I feel nothing but pride for Audrey, she skated so well. She's on her way to do great things.

I skate second and, while my free skate isn't quite as magical as the short skate, I easily take back the first place, and with a comfortable lead. Nicole skates third, and she actually, literally, falls on her butt, dropping to last place. Christine is next, and she maintains herself, coming fourth.

And now the moment of truth: Cicely's free skate. She is a mess. She never had much grace, but she looks stiff. Her transitions are even more awkward than usual. And to top it all off, she misses a triple. If it hadn't been for Nicole's fall, I would have called Cicely's skate the worst of the day.

She had a good enough score on the short skate to maintain her second place, but only just.

During the medal ceremony, Audrey gets bronze, Cicely silver, and I gold. The group insists on taking me out to celebrate after the ceremony, but I am not in a festive mood.

"What is wrong with you? You won!" asks Chuck.

"And Cicely got the second place. There are two female skaters going to the Olympics this year, and it's probably going to be the two of us."

"Ouch," Pierce winces. He's been to the Olympic village. He gets it.

"What are you guys talking about?"

"Didn't you go to college, babe?"

"Yeah, but I don't-"

"And you lived in the rez', right?"

"Yeah. So?"

"Imagine sharing your dorm room with the blond psycho, and that's what the Olympics are going to be like for Anna."

"The life of an Olympian is not glamorous," I add somberly. Everyone agrees that a quiet, commiserating dinner from room service would be better.

CHAPTER 28

On Sunday morning, Anna and I wake up at about eight.

"What time do you have to be at the arena?"

"Eleven. I'm in the second practice group."

"Good, we have time for a room service breakfast. You grab a shower, I'll make the call."

"Hey, you are not the boss of me. As it happens, I would prefer to take a shower now, but don't get it in your head that I'm doing it because you told me to."

We've only been living together, officially, for a month, and it's like that all the time. It's so awesome. I love my girlfriend. Someday I'll marry her.

The shower is still running when I get off the phone with room service, so I turn on the TV for some noise and some company. It happens to play the news, and the news is shocking enough that when they move on to a different subject I turn the TV back off and grab my phone. I need to show this to Anna.

And I do, as soon as she comes out of the shower. "I don't think you have to worry about the Olympics, babe."

"What are you talking about?"

I show her my phone, and the headline: *Cicely Novak disqualified from National Figure Skating Championship for use of performance enhancing drugs!* She goes on to read the rest of the article, which mentions the fight between Cicely and her mom, and the allegations that there was an affair between Cicely and Blaise Darrow.

"Wow," she eventually says. "Mom must be so humiliated."

"Don't tell me you feel sorry for her!"

"Okay, I won't. I'll just say that I don't wish that on anyone, not even her."

I can't say I agree with my girl on this. As far as I can see, her mom got exactly what she deserved. But I'm not going to start an argument about that, I'll just enjoy the karma in private.

***

The five of us are sitting in the arena, ready to cheer for Anna. She told us that she had been preparing a special exhibition number, and that we would love it.

We watch a bunch of other skaters, including the cute little girl who finished in third yesterday. I notice her especially because I guess she's the one who's going to the Olympics with Anna. She looks awfully young for that. She does skate well though, even if she chose a song that played everywhere on the radio last year. It's a theme song for

301

a movie; the movie's decent and the song is okay, it just got overplayed.

And now, finally, it's Anna's turn. She's wearing this blue suit that's made to look like an old fashioned dress, and the black skates that we gave her for her birthday. Her hair is straight, and kept out of her face by a black ribbon. The announcer presents her number, which is apparently called Alice, Underground. She sort of looks like Alice, from the Disney cartoon, but the music doesn't match. It starts as some really disturbing, almost out of tune piano.

From my left, I hear Ava squealing. "It is Alice!"

"What are you talking about?"

"It's that Avril Lavigne song, from the Tim Burton movie. Didn't you watch it?"

"Didn't watch the credits, I bet," answers Chuck, who is sitting next to Ava, before cupping her hands around her mouth and yelling, "Go Anna!"

Ava and I, and the guys, join in. I didn't watch the credits of the Tim Burton movie, so I'm taking Ava's word for it. Anna made us an Alice in Wonderland show. That's so cool!

The most awesome thing is that, while it's a great song for us, it's an even better song for her. Like, the chorus says "When the world's crashing down, when I fall and hit the ground, I will turn myself around," and yeah, she will. I'm so crazy proud of her.

***

The post-Nationals, pre-Olympic month is just as insane as I remember it, crazier, even. The increased press coverage is made worse by the Russian anti-gay laws controversy. The extra training to work out last minute kinks comes with a good helping of studying the competition, which I never used to do when my mom was managing me.

I've been thinking a lot about my mom. She must be feeling terrible, with what happened with Cicely and with that creep husband of hers. She's probably getting a divorce, and she won't be managing anyone's career for a good long time. At least not someone who can afford to avoid her; she didn't do anything, but she's tainted by association. A part of me wants to reach out to her, to give her some support.

I know better, though. She wouldn't see it as support, she would see it as gloating. So I keep to myself, I wait for her to make the first move, or not, and I prepare for the Olympics.

The flight is much longer from Winnipeg to Sochi than from Toronto to Vancouver, and the jetlag is much more intense. The opening ceremony, the interviews, the training, even the Short Skate just fly by. The Short Skate did not go as well as during the Nationals, but I'm okay with that. My National Short Skate was a special moment for me, and failing to repeat it doesn't break my heart.

And now, I am walking across the Olympic village as the light of dawn washes over Russia. I have no idea what time it is back home, I forgot to look it up. In a few hours, I will skate my Free Skate, my last competitive skate in the Olympics. Perhaps my last competitive skate ever, if I'm not invited to participate in the World Championship.

After over a year of racking my brains over this, over a year of false alerts, I am now truly ready to take the next step in my life. I want to continue skating, but I'm done with competition. I don't need it anymore, I've proven myself. I'll join the pros this summer, make contacts, to prepare myself for the step after pro-skating: choreography. And with all of that, I want to go back to Winnipeg, my hometown. I want to be with my friends, with my boyfriend. I want to marry Luke, and maybe even have his children when the time is right.

I am ready for the future.

It is with that state of mind that I take the ice for my free skate. My past is settled, my future is open and friendly, and now, right now, I am completely in the present. I take my place at the center of the ice, and there is nothing but me, the ice, and the music.

And I skate.

EPILOGUE

**April 2014 (Associated Press)**

Susanna Miles, four-time World Champion and gold medalist of the Sochi Olympics, announced yesterday that she is retiring from competition. Miss Miles announced that she is joining Stars on Ice. More inside.

**June 2015**

You are cordially invited to the wedding of Susanna Miles and Lucas Crawford, Saturday June 20th, 2:30 PM, at the Le Cercle Moliere Theater. RSVP

**April 2017 (Associated Press)**

Audrey Lennon wins the World Championship, with a routine choreographed by former World Champion and Olympian Susanna Miles-Crawford.

The Winnipeg Jets win the Stanley Cup, led by team captain Lucas Crawford, who also led team Canada to a gold medal earlier this year.

Email

From: Olivia Bristol
To: Susanna Miles-Crawford
September 3rd 2023, at 8:40

[attachment]

Susanna, you need to come to Toronto. I have a new skater, one who I believe shows great promise. She needs the best of everything, including the best choreography, and that means you. I'm joining all the necessary details in an attachment.

Email

From: Susanna Miles-Crawford
To: Olivia Bristol
September 3rd, 2023, at 9:15

Mother, I'm very happy for you, but I must insist: I believe it would be best for us both not to associate on a professional level.

Congratulations on the marriage, by the way. Hopefully the third time is the charm.

Email

From: Olivia Bristol
To: Susanna Miles-Crawford
September 3rd 2023, at 8:40

[EMAIL MARKED AS SPAM]

June 2030 (Associated Press)

Lucas Crawford announced his retirement from the National Hockey League. Crawford, who led the Jets to three Stanley Cups during his career as team captain, has accepted a coaching position for his Alma Mater, the University of Moncton. The exact date of the departure of Crawford, his wife - gold medalist from the Sochi Olympics and former World Champion of figure skating, Susanna Miles-Crawford - and their two children is unknown. But certainly, their absence will leave a hole in their community, and in the city of Winnipeg.

ACKNOWLEDGEMENTS

I offer thanks to:

- My family, a constant source of comfort and inspiration;

- My friends Caro, Manon and Marie-Claude, my first audience;

- Brendan Butt and Karine Gauthier, who generously offered to model for the cover;

- Chris Baty, who created Nanowrimo, of which this novel is a product;

- The wonderful team at Renaissance Press who took this revised, but still raw, Nanowrimo project and made it into the book you are reading today. Which leads me to, last but not least:

- You, whoever you are, because you've read the book all the way to the end. Something I wrote kept you engaged all the way to the bottom cover, and I can't describe how amazing this feels.